Welcome to the Secret World of Alex Mack!

I thought it would be a piece of cake to earn some extra money working at the local grocery store. But when my mom's surprise cake was stuck in the back of the walk-in freezer behind a huge shipment of ice, I morphed my way to the back of the freezer. Annie wouldn't approve, but I didn't expect to get locked inside, and I definitely didn't know I'd become a frozen ice cube myself. Even worse, those other blocks of ice belong to the chemical plant, and now we're all headed for the lab. Talk about chills! Let me explain. . . .

I'm Alex Mack. I was just another average kid until my first day of junior high.

One minute I'm walking home from school—the next there's a *crash!* A truck from the Paradise Valley Chemical plant overturns in front of me, and I'm drenched in some weird chemical.

And since then—well, nothing's been the same. I can move objects with my mind, shoot electrical charges through my fingertips, and morph into a liquid shape . . . which is handy when I get in a tight spot!

My best friend, Ray, thinks it's cool—and my sister, Annie, thinks I'm a science project.

They're the only two people who know about my new powers. I can't let anyone else find out—not even my parents—because I know the chemical plant wants to find me and turn me into some experiment.

But you know something? I guess I'm not so average anymore!

The Secret World of Alex Mack™

Alex, You're Glowing!
Bet You Can't!
Bad News Babysitting!
Witch Hunt!
Mistaken Identity!
Cleanup Catastrophe!
Take a Hike!
Go for the Gold!
Poison in Paradise!
Super Edition: Zappy Holidays!
Junkyard Jitters!
Frozen Stiff!

Available from MINSTREL Books

the secret world of

ALEX MACK ™

Frozen Stiff!

Diana G. Gallagher

A MINSTREL® BOOK

Published by POCKET BOOKS
New York   London   Toronto   Sydney   Tokyo   Singapore

A MINSTREL PAPERBACK *Original*

 A Minstrel Book published by
POCKET BOOKS, a division of Simon & Schuster Inc.
1230 Avenue of the Americas, New York, NY 10020

ISBN: 0-671-00281-3

First Minstrel Books printing February 1997

10 9 8 7 6 5 4 3 2 1

Cover photography by Thomas Queally and Danny Feld

Printed in the U.S.A.

To Brandon Isbell
with many thanks for sharing
insights and experiences
that added so much to this book

Frozen Stiff!

CHAPTER 1

"Would you like me to help you out with these bags, ma'am?" Alex Mack asked the customer at the checkout counter.

"Yes, please." The elderly woman watched closely as Alex placed a loaf of bread on top of the paper products already in the brown paper sack. Plastic bags were easier to fill and carry, but the woman had asked for paper.

Smiling, Alex carefully put the bag in a shopping cart. The one bit of advice her mother had given her before she started working at the grocery store three days ago had been short and to the point.

1

Don't squash the bread!

It was sound advice. Alex had just finished two afternoons of training at the Plaza Market, and it hadn't taken her long to realize that almost every customer watched to make certain the bread wasn't crunched under heavier items.

Her third training shift had been cancelled when one of the full-time baggers had called in sick. School was closed for students because of a teacher planning day, and Mr. Lindsey had offered her the extra hours doing the real thing.

Adjusting her ponytail holder, Alex stepped back to let the woman walk ahead and noticed the store manager watching her intently. Mr. Lindsey had made it quite clear that he did not tolerate anyone who didn't take their duties seriously. He was not unkind—just dedicated to providing first-rate customer service. Damaging the merchandise was the worst offense a bagger could commit. However, Alex had been careful not to set any bags on top of other bags in the cart. The manager gave her a curt nod of approval and Alex relaxed as she followed the customer to the exit.

Alex's bank account had been decreasing steadily since Paradise Valley Video had closed.

The physical work at the market was harder than her job at the video store, but Alex was thrilled to be employed again. She had gotten used to having her own money to spend any way she wanted, and there were more teenagers looking for jobs than there were jobs in Paradise Valley. Mr. Lindsey had hired her because Mrs. Hardwick, the owner of the video store, had given her a glowing reference. Alex was determined to prove he had made the right choice.

"My car is right over there." The woman pointed to a blue, compact wagon in the middle of the parking lot as she approached the automatic door.

Ray Alvarado dashed through the in-door and stopped short. "Alex! I've been looking all over for you—"

"Hi—" Alex glanced back at the customer service counter. Mr. Lindsey was still watching her—and scowling. Talking with friends instead of paying attention to business was also high on his list of employee *do nots*. "Can't talk now, Ray." Alex kept walking through the open door.

"But—"

Alex didn't want to be so abrupt with her best

3

friend, but she was on the time clock. The Plaza Market was paying for her time and attention.

The old woman walked ever-so-slowly across the parking lot, and Alex patiently held back to stay behind her. When they finally reached the car, she waited while the woman unlocked and raised the hatchback.

"I think everything will fit back here." Fumbling with her keys, the gray-haired woman turned away.

Alex let go of the shopping cart and picked up a bag. As she turned to set the bag in the car, the cart began to roll forward on the sloping pavement. The elderly customer was opening the front door and didn't notice. Alex gasped, realizing that the cart was going to run into her.

With her arms full of groceries, Alex couldn't grab it with her hand. She threw an electromagnetic force field between the cart and the woman. The cart bumped into the invisible barrier, then swerved toward the back door.

Alex instantly latched onto the cart handle with a telekinetic thought, stopping the crash and saving the blue paint from being scratched. Then, shifting the heavy bag into one arm, Alex placed her other hand on the handle just as the

4

woman looked back. The wrinkles in her face deepened in a worried frown.

"Are you sure you can manage this, dear?"

"Oh, yes! No problem." Clutching the grocery sack, Alex slowly pulled the cart back. Afraid to let go again, she bent her knees and stooped to put the bag in the car. The heavy, unbalanced sack overturned as she set it down and several cans of vegetables rolled out.

"Sorry," Alex mumbled as she righted the bag and gathered the cans with her free hand. Her mind raced. There had to be a solution to the runaway cart problem other than holding it in place with a force field or telekinesis. All the other baggers managed without powers, but no one had given her lessons in cart control. Then she saw a crack in the pavement. She positioned the front wheels in the depression, and the cart stayed put.

Satisfied, the old woman sighed and slipped into the driver's seat.

After Alex finished loading the groceries, she closed the hatchback and turned to see Mr. Lindsey staring at her through the large, front window. *Just great*, Alex thought as she pushed the cart back toward the store. The manager, of course, didn't have a clue that she had averted disaster with her fantastic powers. As far as he was concerned, dumb luck had saved the old woman and her car from the stampeding shopping cart. However, Alex was confident she could explain. Now that she knew the carts had to be placed just right on the paved inclines, she wouldn't make the same mistake again. Certainly, Mr. Lindsey would understand.

Maybe. Through the window Alex saw the manager shake his head. He was about to turn away when Ray intercepted her halfway to the door.

"I thought you had today off, Alex." Ray fell into step beside her.

"I did, but someone called in sick." Alex kept moving as she talked. She couldn't brush Ray off a second time, but she didn't want to get fired, either. Spotting two shopping carts on the walk in front of the store, she steered toward them.

"So when do you get off?" Ray helped as Alex shoved all three carts together.

"Six."

"Too bad. *Super Cop Two* will be gone from the theater after today."

Alex looked up sharply. "I forgot we were supposed to go to a matinee."

"We could catch the twilight show at six-thirty," Ray suggested hopefully. "That's still matinee prices."

"Can't," Alex said as she pushed the carts toward the door. "I promised Nicole I'd help sell sodas at the rally before the high school's big basketball game with Pleasant View High. The rally starts at six-thirty." Alex shrugged apologetically and paused before triggering the automatic door. "The profits go to our class charity."

"Don't worry about it. I'd rather go to the game and root for Paradise Valley's varsity team anyway. If they win, they'll be in the county play-offs and on their way to the State Championship. The movie will be out on video in a few months. We'll rent it."

"My treat," Alex offered. "But if I don't get back to work, I'll lose my job and I won't be able to afford it."

"Catch ya at the game."

Alex waved over her shoulder and shoved the carts through the opening door.

Mr. Lindsey was waiting for her when she returned to the checkout. "Not exactly record-breaking time getting back in from outside."

"I'm sorry, Mr. Lindsey. I was getting those carts—"

"And having a parking lot conference with a friend."

"Yes, but I didn't—"

"Come with me, Alex," Mr. Lindsey ordered sternly.

"But—" Alex didn't have a chance to explain. The manager turned and walked away. Certain she had just bumbled herself into the ranks of the unemployed, Alex sighed and followed.

Fired at fifteen! She'd never live down the humiliation!

CHAPTER 2

As Alex trudged past the rows of checkout counters on Mr. Lindsey's heels the other baggers and checkers glanced at her with grim expressions. The golden glow of embarrassment warmed her cheeks. Hanging her head and shielding her face with her hand, Alex breathed in deeply and tried to calm herself.

Losing a job isn't the end of the world. Besides, who wants to work for someone who can't forgive an honest mistake?

I do, Alex answered herself. This was the only job she had been offered since the video store closed. In addition to the financial independence a paycheck provided, getting paid for a job well done gave her a sense of accomplishment and self-respect. Mrs. Hardwick had been an understanding and appreciative boss, but maybe she was the exception. The Plaza Market was a much bigger and busier enterprise than the video store. It employed over a hundred people. The management didn't have to tolerate mistakes or accept excuses, even when there were good reasons. Anyone who didn't measure up was easily replaced. Alex's parents and sister were constant reminders of just how tough and ruthless the working world could be.

Her mom was a victim of corporate downsizing. Mrs. Mack had been the account executive for Paradise Valley Chemical, a public relations position that forced her to deal with the company's demanding CEO. However, even though she had done a fantastic job of promoting Danielle Atron and the plant, she had still been laid off when the PR firm was restructured. It was totally unfair, but boosting a dwindling profit margin had been more important to the company than keeping a loyal, hardworking employee.

Mr. Mack had worked at Paradise Valley

Chemical for years. He was paid well, but he was constantly under pressure to produce results. The stress had increased a lot since Danielle Atron hired Lars Fredrickson to work with him on GC-161, the experimental compound that had endowed Alex with her secret powers. Alex's father still didn't know how the company planned to use and market the substance. Worse, although her father suspected the gene-altering chemical might be illegal and harmful, he couldn't do anything about it. He couldn't risk losing his job on a hunch that might be wrong, especially now that her mother was unemployed and going to school to get her master's degree in social work.

Even Alex's sister, Annie, worked at Paradise Valley Chemical now. Although she was just an intern and not officially involved in any of the plant's secret projects, she still had to deal with the same pressures and moral questions as their father. For one thing, Annie had been studying the effects of GC-161 on her younger sister for a long time. She *knew* just how potent and dangerous the compound might be. If Danielle Atron found out Annie was using her job to advance her own GC-161 research, she'd be fired in a hurry, too.

The threat of losing a job was always there, Alex realized, but knowing that didn't soften the blow.

Alex was so lost in thought, she almost didn't notice when Mr. Lindsey stopped abruptly. She barely avoided a collision with him.

"This is the produce section." Without turning around, Mr. Lindsey paused to survey the bins of fruits and vegetables lining the aisles.

Surprise and confusion instantly subdued Alex's anxiety, and the golden flush on her cheeks faded before the manager looked back at her.

"It's not too busy right now, so you might as well learn how to stock."

"Stock? You mean I'm not fired?" Alex blurted out the question.

"No, not yet." Mr. Lindsey almost smiled. He coughed and eyed her pointedly instead. "However, if you make a habit of hanging out with your friends on store time—"

"I won't," Alex quickly interjected.

"See that you don't. Now—a word of advice about Mrs. Argyle."

"Mrs. Argyle?" Alex asked anxiously.

"The produce manager. As far as she's concerned, fruits and vegetables should be treated with the same care as fine china. Mrs. Argyle is very nice—until she catches someone playing slam-dunk with the oranges or squashing tomatoes. So don't drop anything."

Nodding, Alex followed Mr. Lindsey through swinging double doors into a huge storeroom. He left after introducing her to Mrs. Argyle.

Eager to please, Alex listened attentively as the plump and pleasant woman gave her a quick tour of the warehouse. Boxed and canned items were kept in the main area. Two large coolers for produce and dairy products and a huge freezer lined the back wall. Then Mrs. Argyle handed Alex an apron and put her to work stacking wooden crates of lettuce onto a large dolly. When the dolly was loaded, Alex pushed it out into the aisle where Mrs. Argyle was waiting with a shopping cart.

"We rotate everything in the store when we put out new stock," Mrs. Argyle said. "But it's especially important in the produce section. Produce wilts and rots."

Alex blinked. "Rotate?"

Mrs. Argyle smiled patiently. "Take the old lettuce out of the bin and put it in the shopping cart. Then put the new heads in the bin at the back and on the bottom. When that's done, put the old ones back so they're on the top and toward the front. That way the older produce won't be sitting on the bottom getting too old to sell."

"I get it!" Alex grinned. "So that's why my mom is always picking things out from the back."

"She does, huh?" Mrs. Argyle winked. "So do I, but a lot of our customers are too rushed to take the time. So for the most part, rotation works."

"Yeah. My dad just grabs and runs. He wants to get in and out of the store as fast as he can."

Mrs. Argyle nodded. "If you should find something that looks really gross, bring it to the back and we'll trash it. Some of our stock people aren't quite as particular about the market's reputation for having fresh, quality produce as they should be."

"I'll be careful." Without waiting to be told, Alex began removing heads of lettuce from the bin and gently placing them in the shopping cart.

Mrs. Argyle watched her like a hawk for a minute, then smiled. "One more thing. If it gets busier and they call you to the checkout—go immediately."

"Okay."

Alex worked diligently and without mishap for the next half hour. The store wasn't too busy, but a few customers stopped to take fresh lettuce from the crates. One woman examined a dozen heads Alex had already stocked before deciding on the perfect choice, but she apologized for disrupting the orderly bin as she moved on to onions. Mr. Hernandez, an elderly man who worked at the deli counter, took a moment to introduce himself and compliment her work. Harvey Jenkins, a high-school boy, stopped on his way to the dairy counter with a load of cheese and margarine to offer assistance if she needed it. By the time all the lettuce had been stocked, Alex felt more at ease and she returned to the storeroom determined not to let the incident in the parking lot overshadow her job performance.

Mrs. Argyle was busy inspecting a shipment of fruit that had just arrived and directed Alex to stock tomatoes next. Remembering Mr. Lindsey's warning, Alex loaded the cardboard boxes with extra care and headed for the produce aisle. However, as she began lifting the half-filled boxes of older tomatoes out of the display case, her name was called over the P.A. system.

Alex hesitated, wondering if she should leave the dolly full of boxes in the aisle or take it back to the storeroom.

"Alex to checkout number six. Now, please!"

Leaving the dolly, Alex hurried to the checkout counter to bag groceries for a sudden rush of customers. When she returned twenty minutes later, she skidded to a halt and stared at the tomato bin in shock. A grade-school boy wearing a red baseball cap and a red jacket was pounding tomatoes to a pulp with an ear of corn. His mother was nowhere in sight. No one else was around to witness the incident, either.

"Hey!" Alex dashed forward. "Stop that!"

The boy stuck out his tongue, picked up a dripping tomato, and threw it at her. His actions were so unexpected and happened so quickly, Alex was too surprised to do anything except duck.

But she didn't duck fast enough.

The broken tomato hit the hollow of her shoulder with a squishing *splat!* Tomato juice and pulp sprayed over the top of her T-shirt, the front of her apron, and her face.

Sputtering, she watched as the boy tossed the corn into the green pepper bin, then ran around the end of the aisle. More concerned with the condition of Mrs. Argyle's precious tomatoes than her own appearance, Alex dashed to the bin. Groaning, she lifted the cardboard box nearest the front of the bin and stared at it. A dozen pulverized tomatoes lay in a red-pulp puddle. Juice began to seep through the soggy bottom of the box.

It could be worse, Alex told herself. At least the boy had confined his tomato smashing rampage to one box of old tomatoes. Still, she wasn't sure how she was going to explain the damage. What if Mrs. Argyle didn't believe that an unattended child had committed the unpardonable crime of tomato demolition?

Projecting a small electromagnetic force field under the box to keep the juice from dripping on the floor, Alex turned to set the box down on the end of the dolly.

"Alex Mack!"

Startled by the sound of Kelly Phillips's voice, Alex dropped the box, telekinetically grabbed it without thinking, then instantly let it finish its fall. It hit the edge of the dolly and landed upside down on the floor. More juice, pulp, and seeds splashed onto Alex's shoes and jeans.

"I didn't know you worked here." Smiling sweetly, Kelly paused to look at the box, then back at Alex. She was holding a bottle of expensive sparkling water and wearing a spotless, white tennis outfit. She had obviously stopped to buy the water on her way to the courts at the Paradise Valley Country Club.

Alex hesitated. Had the girl seen the box stop falling for that brief moment? Kelly was determined to prove that there was something inexplicably strange about Alex Mack. After two years, Danielle Atron, convinced that the GC-161 kid did not pose a threat to the project, had given up trying to identify her. However, even a hint about her unusual abilities might prompt the plant CEO to start looking again. At the moment, though, Kelly seemed more interested in Alex's job at the market than in gathering evidence to support her "Alex-is-weird" theory.

"Are you a stock person, Alex?"

"I can't talk now, Kelly." Squatting, Alex turned the box right side up. It wasn't easy maintaining her dignity while covered with squashed tomato stuff and scooping broken tomatoes off the floor with her bare hands, but Alex was determined to stay composed. "I've got work to do."

"Oh, of course." Kelly nodded, looking concerned. "I think it's really commendable that you're willing to work at such a dirty job to help your family out in hard times. I mean, now that your mom is unemployed and everything."

Alex fumed. "I'm working here because *I* want to, Kelly. It doesn't have anything to do with—"

"What happened here?" Mrs. Argyle snapped loudly as she came out of the storeroom and saw the ruined tomatoes on the floor.

At the same moment, Mr. Lindsey walked out from the next aisle. His narrowed gaze flicked between Kelly and Alex.

"I'm late for my tennis lesson, and I still have to pay for this." Kelly held up the bottle. "See you later."

Mrs. Argyle and Mr. Lindsey started toward Alex from opposite directions.

Alex sighed heavily as Kelly walked away. *There's no way out of this one*, she thought dismally. It looked as if she had broken two rules within an hour of being warned.

She had literally been caught red-handed with a dropped box of destroyed tomatoes.

And the manager had seen her talking to Kelly.

Losing her job because she was talking to a real friend like Ray would be bad enough.

Getting fired for talking to Kelly would just add insult to injury.

CHAPTER 3

Alex held her head high as Mr. Lindsey and Mrs. Argyle stopped in front of her. The truth was her only defense.

Mrs. Argyle silently stared at the mess on the floor, shaking her head in dismay.

"Friend of yours?" Mr. Lindsey asked with a glance at Kelly's departing back.

"No, sir," Alex answered honestly. Kelly Phillips was not her friend. Even though the girl always acted nice, Alex knew Kelly was a selfish and scheming fake. *And I'm her favorite target.* "She just asked me a question." *Also true.* As long as Mr. Lindsey didn't ask *what* question, he wouldn't know the conversation had been personal.

The store manager didn't ask. Satisfied, Mr. Lindsey nodded, then turned his attention to the puddle of lumpy tomato puree on the floor. "What happened here?"

"You were being so careful, Alex." Mrs. Argyle's eyes clouded with disappointment. "But this wasn't an accident. It looks like someone went on a tomato-smashing spree."

"Someone did, but it wasn't me," Alex said calmly. "When I came back from the checkout, I found this little boy beating the tomatoes with an ear of corn." Alex pointed to the battered ear lying on top of the green peppers. "I know it sounds lame, but—"

"Chucky Randall." Mr. Lindsey and Mrs. Argyle spoke in unison and looked at each other knowingly.

"Was he about nine years old and wearing a red cap and jacket?" Mr. Lindsey asked.

Alex nodded.

"I'll handle it." Sighing, Mr. Lindsey hurried away to find the young culprit.

"You know him?" Alex asked, relieved.

"Yes, I do. Chucky's not a bad kid," Mrs. Argyle said without conviction. "He's just very smart, full of energy, and too curious for his own good. His mother does her best to keep track of him, but he's so bright, he occasionally gives her the slip. He'll probably grow up to be a world-famous rocket scientist or something."

Alex smiled. "I was afraid you'd blame me."

"Everyone makes mistakes, especially when they first start. But you're doing fine, Alex. I'll help you clean up this mess, then you could use some cleaning up yourself."

Alex grimaced as she gazed down at the tomato stains on her shirt, apron, and jeans. She was filthy and her hands, arms, and face were sticky with tomato splatterings. She had planned on going directly to the basketball rally after getting off work. Now she'd have to go home and change first.

"Nothing that can't be fixed," Mrs. Argyle assured her. "Some soap and water and a clean apron will make a big difference. "You're about due for a break anyway."

"Thanks, but after we take care of the floor, maybe I should finish stocking the tomatoes—before anything else happens to them."

Mrs. Argyle beamed. "That's very responsible

of you, Alex, but Harvey can do it. You'll feel better after you've washed up. Take a half hour and get yourself a snack.''

When the floor was clean, Alex rinsed the mop and bucket, dumped the dirty apron in a laundry bag and grabbed a clean one. As she headed for the employee restrooms, she felt certain that if she could just make it to the end of her shift without something else going wrong, everything would be fine.

But that was a big *if.* Disaster seemed to be dogging her with a tenacious determination today, and she was only barely managing to keep one step ahead of it.

Annie Mack sat bolt upright in her chair as alarms clanged in the halls throughout the plant.

Kaa-lannng! Klang, Klang!

What's going on? Annie's mind raced as she tried to remember what that particular siren pattern meant. *A fire drill?* Her eyes widened and her palms began to sweat as another, more sinister possibility entered her mind. *Maybe there was a leak in a dangerous, experimental chemical tank. . . .*

Saving the lab information she had just entered into the computer database, Annie jumped up as her father rushed in from the hall.

"Don't panic, Annie." Holding up his hands, Mr. Mack smiled reassuringly. "That's just a code-two alarm."

"Equipment failure, right?" Annie asked, surprised to hear a tremor in her voice.

"That's right! You really did study the employee manual, didn't you?"

Annie nodded. "But it's not—"

"Toxic contamination?" Mr. Mack shook his head. "No. Just an ordinary maintenance priority call. Nothing to worry about."

Annie looked beyond him to see several maintenance people race past the open door. Judging by their tense expressions and haste, she couldn't help but wonder just how *ordinary* the equipment failure really was.

The alarms shut off abruptly.

Mr. Mack glanced at his watch. "It's after one-thirty and you haven't gone to lunch yet, have you? Don't you have your car keys?"

"Uh, no, I mean—yes. I've got my keys, but I didn't want to leave without finishing the file I was entering."

Actually, Annie had asked to use the car and

had postponed going to lunch so she could stop by Brewster's Sweet Shoppe. Her mother had ordered an ice cream cake to surprise her father, but she couldn't pick it up herself. Her mom had classes until six and the shop would be closed by the time she got there.

There wasn't any special occasion. Her mother just wanted to do something nice to thank her husband for being so supportive of her decision to return to school. It was Friday and she had made dinner reservations at his favorite Chinese restaurant. The evening would be topped off with ice cream cake and coffee at home.

Now, as Annie saw Lars Fredrickson charge past the door after the maintenance crew, she wished she hadn't agreed to run the errand. Something big was happening, and it might be related to GC-161. The European chemist had been hired specifically to work with her father on the compound.

Mr. Mack leaned out the door. "Hey, Lars! What's happening?"

"Nothing that concerns you, Mack!" The chemist's voice echoed down the hall.

Shrugging, Mr. Mack looked back at Annie. "I really appreciate you spending your day off from school working, Annie, but you've got to eat."

"But—"

"That's an order . . . from your boss." Mr. Mack grinned as he ducked out the door. "Just be back in an hour."

Reluctantly, Annie closed the computer files and picked up her purse. The cake would be done at two. Even with the car, she'd have to rush to pick it up, take it home and put it in the freezer, then return to the plant on time.

Annie paused in the doorway to avoid being trampled by a frantic team of technicians storming toward the research and development complex. Then, as she hurried down the hall to the lobby, she heard Lars shouting orders into a cellular phone.

"Fifteen minutes! No more. Timing is absolutely critical. The success of this experiment could change the lives of desperate people everywhere!"

Desperate people everywhere? Annie thought. She was certain the maintenance emergency involved GC-161. The compound was being developed so people could lose weight and keep the pounds off without exercising. It was the biggest, most important and potentially profitable project Paradise Valley Chemical had going.

Nothing else could throw the plant into such a panic.

And, Annie realized with a growing sense of apprehension, anything that concerned GC-161 concerned her sister, Alex. Given the plant's sophisticated equipment and unlimited resources, there was always a chance Lars would discover something about the compound that had eluded her . . . something that might endanger her younger sister. The sooner she got back to the plant, the better her chances of finding out if there was any reason to worry.

Annie ran across the parking lot.

CHAPTER 4

After her break, Alex tackled lemons feeling much more relaxed. In spite of the tomato fiasco, Mrs. Argyle knew it wasn't her fault and left her to work without supervision.

As she cleared the top layer of old lemons, Alex realized the underlying fruits had been there a long time. *Way too long.* The yellow skins were covered with brown spots. Some of the lemons were disgustingly soft and squishy. Whoever had been stocking them had *not* been rotating. Mrs. Argyle wouldn't be pleased when Alex brought her a crate of rotted fruit, but she'd be less pleased if a customer discovered the spoiled produce.

Alex grabbed an empty crate from the store-room, then went to the front of the store for another shopping cart. Just as she turned to head back, Annie burst through the automatic doors carrying a white box.

"Alex! I need a favor—"

Holding her finger to her lips, Alex quickly glanced around. There was a midafternoon lull in business, and Mr. Lindsey was hunched over a computer at the customer service counter. Waving Annie to follow, Alex hustled back to the produce section with the cart.

"I thought you were working today, Annie." Alex began removing the rotted lemons as she talked.

"I am, but I had to run an errand for Mom on my lunch hour. Listen—" Annie lowered her voice. "Some kind of equipment failure alarm went off at the plant a while ago that totally freaked Lars. I don't know if it has anything to do with GC-161, but I've got to get back right away to find out."

Alex paused. "So what are you doing here?"

"I had to wait an extra fifteen minutes for this ice cream cake Mom ordered for Dad. If I take it home, I'll be late getting back to work and I can't take it with me 'cause it'll melt." Annie held the box out to Alex.

"What am I supposed to do with it? I don't get off until six."

Exasperated, Annie rolled her eyes. "Doesn't this store have a freezer?"

Alex nodded. "Sure. There's a huge one in the storeroom, but—"

"So put it in the freezer until you clock out. Then take it home. It's the perfect solution."

Alex stared at the white box. The receipt was taped to the top and Brewster's Sweet Shoppe was printed on the top and sides in bold, black letters. "I can't, Annie!"

"Why not?"

"It's not from this store! You wouldn't believe the day I've been having. If Mr. Lindsey catches me doing *anything* that's against the rules—"

"I don't have time to argue, Alex." Annie set the cake box beside the crate in the shopping cart. "I'm about to go snooping around the plant to find out if something happened that might affect *your* welfare. The least you can do is stash this cake for Mom. It's frozen solid now, but I wouldn't wait too long to get it into a freezer."

Alex relented with a nod. "Okay. I have to go

home and change before I go to the game rally at school, anyway."

"Great. I gotta go."

"Be careful, Annie."

"I will." Spinning about, Annie jogged around the end of the aisle and was gone.

Alex quickly scooped the rest of the damaged lemons out of the bin and into the crate. She didn't know if storing merchandise from other stores was a violation of company policy or not. If she asked and the answer was "no," she'd only have two choices. Let the cake melt or store it in the freezer anyway and risk getting caught deliberately breaking another rule. If she didn't ask, she could save the cake and plead ignorance if Mr. Lindsey found out.

Alex decided not to ask. Dealing with the cake was a complication she really didn't need, but Annie might be walking into even bigger trouble at Paradise Valley Chemical. There wasn't anything she could do to help except wait and hope that the problem at the plant didn't have anything to do with GC-161 or her.

Hoping Mrs. Argyle wouldn't notice the white box from Brewster's resting beside the lemon crate, Alex wheeled the shopping cart toward the storeroom.

"Yo! Alex!"

Ray? Alex couldn't believe it when she looked over her shoulder and saw Nicole, Robyn, Ray, and Louis waving as they hurried toward her. Stopping the cart, she turned around and sagged as they formed a semicircle in front of her.

"How's the job going, Alex?" Robyn asked.

"Fine, but—"

"How'd you get red stuff all over your shirt?" Louis asked. "It looks totally gross."

"It's a long story, but I can't—"

"You're still coming to help out at the rally, aren't you?" Nicole asked with a worried frown.

Alex nodded. "I'll be a little late because I have to go home and change, but I'll be there—"

"That's good because Katy Robertson got sick and had to back out," Robyn said.

"So I volunteered to take her place." Ray grinned.

"And volunteered my services, too," Louis added. "Now we'll have to wait six months for *Super Cop Two* to show up on video to see it."

"Uh-huh. Listen, guys, I can't talk—"

Too late. Alex's heart sank when she saw Mr.

Lindsey marching down the aisle. If she didn't know better, she'd think there was a cosmic conspiracy at work to make sure she lost her job. And her mother's cake, too. A mental image of the frozen dessert thawing into a blob of ice cream cake mush spurred her to action.

With her back still pressed against the cart handle, Alex took a backward step toward the storeroom. "Sorry, but I've got some things to take care of—"

"Just a minute, Alex!" Mr. Lindsey called out.

Alex froze as the store manager joined the line in front of her. Her body was blocking his view of the cart, and she didn't think he could see the cake box. *Not that it matters much now,* she thought miserably.

"Hi, kids." Mr. Lindsey smiled and shook Nicole's hand. "Is Alex a friend of yours?"

"One of my best friends." Nicole beamed. "She's working with us at the basketball rally, too."

"Really?" Cupping his chin thoughtfully, Mr. Lindsey looked at Alex and sighed. "Well, in that case, I don't have any choice but to—"

Alex tensed, waiting to hear the dreaded words.

"—give you the ten percent employee discount."

Employee discount? Alex blinked.

"Ten percent!" Nicole's smile widened. "That'll really help the class charity! Thank you, Mr. Lindsey!"

"On the ice, too?" Louis asked. "Or just the soda?"

Robyn jabbed Louis with her elbow.

Mr. Lindsey grinned. "On the ice, too."

Alex was too dumbfounded to move.

"I've got your cases of soda set aside up front." As Mr. Lindsey ushered the kids ahead of him, he glanced back at Alex. "Back to work." Then, he smiled.

"Right away."

Alex pushed the cart toward the double doors feeling slightly dazed. Mr. Lindsey had given her a lot to think about. The owner of Plaza Market had hired him to run the store. It was his job to make sure the employees didn't goof off and earned the money they were paid. Looking at the spotted lemons in the crate, Alex realized that wasn't always easy. So Mr. Lindsey acted tough even though he was a really nice man. *He* had probably bent the rules by giving the class

Alex's employee discount. It was a generous thing to do, and Alex couldn't help feeling guilty about secretly storing the cake in the company freezer.

But the cake was important to her mom and dad and Annie, and Alex couldn't let them down, either. Even so, taking care of her personal business didn't have to cost the store anything. She'd skip her second break to make up for the minute or two she spent in the freezer.

Harvey was on his way out the double doors with a stack of plastic bags for the checkout counters. He brushed his unruly brown hair off his forehead and wrinkled his nose when he saw the lemons. "Bet Richie did that."

"Who's Richie?" Alex asked innocently, studying the tall, thin boy's angular face.

"He doesn't work here anymore. No surprise, huh?" Winking, Harvey held a door open for her. "Everything going okay, Alex?"

"Great!" Alex didn't know if Harvey had noticed the box from Brewster's Sweet Shoppe, but if he did, she didn't think he'd say anything. Now all she had to do was get past Mrs. Argyle.

As she entered the storeroom, Alex felt a huge rush of astonished relief. Something was finally going right! Mrs. Argyle was in her office—on the far side of the huge room opposite the coolers and freezer. Sitting at her desk with her back turned, the produce manager was nodding vigorously as she talked on the phone.

Steering the cart across the room, Alex parked it behind a tower of empty pallets by the freezer. The three-foot-square, flat wooden pallets looked like squashed packing crates. Suppliers delivered them to the store loaded with everything from bags of dog food to cardboard flats of canned goods. When they were unpacked, the empties were stacked to be returned. Picking up the cake, Alex peeked around the corner of the wooden platforms.

The sound of sirens on the street captured Mrs. Argyle's attention. As the produce manager dashed out of her office to look through a window by the loading dock, Alex sprang to the freezer and yanked open the heavy metal door. Long strips of thick plastic hung down over the doorway to help maintain the interior temperature while the door was open. Alex slipped through them and pulled the door so it stayed slightly ajar. When it closed all the way, it depressed a button that turned off the overhead light inside.

However, hiding the cake wasn't going to be easy. Cardboard boxes full of frozen pizzas, vegetables, and other nuke-and-eat foods were stacked from floor to ceiling along the walls.

Shivering, Alex went to the far end of the walk-in. She set the cake on the floor and reached up to lift a cardboard carton down from the stack in the corner. An ordinary shipping carton sitting alone on the floor wouldn't look out of place and nobody would be able to see the cake box stashed that high up unless they were looking right at it.

Grunting, Alex tugged on the brown box labeled "frozen orange juice concentrate" until half of it extended off the shelf.

Then she heard the screech of the loading door being raised and a man barking orders in the storeroom.

Alex pulled the carton into her arms to lower it down.

The box was heavier than she expected.

"Move it!" the man shouted. "Every second counts!"

The carton slipped from Alex's grasp and fell—directly over the cake.

Reacting on instincts developed after having her powers for more than two years, Alex telekinetically snatched the cake box out of harm's way.

The orange juice carton landed on the floor with a loud thud.

Alex reached out to grab the hovering cake box.

The freezer door was thrown open.

And a man in a blue Paradise Valley Chemical uniform barged through the plastic strips.

CHAPTER 5

"I'm back." Annie stepped into her father's office and paused to catch her breath. The five-minute ride back to the plant had taken fifteen and she had run all the way from the parking lot.

Mr. Mack glanced at the clock on the wall. "You're ten minutes late."

"Yeah, I know." Annie was hoping her father had learned more about the equipment failure. Getting the story from him would save her a lot of time and trouble. But drawing him into a casual conversation wouldn't be easy if he was upset with her.

"You didn't have trouble with the car, did you?" Mr. Mack asked, suddenly worried.

"No. The police have all the main streets blocked off. So I had to take a bunch of detours—along with everyone else driving around town." Annie raised her hands in a gesture of helplessness. "Traffic was backed up a mile. I'm really sorry."

"Actually, the plant was responsible for the roadblocks and the traffic jam, but—" Mr. Mack sighed and rubbed his chin.

Annie looked up sharply. *Why* had the police agreed to close down public streets for the plant? Maybe there was a connection to the alarm that went off earlier.

"The *plant* did that? How come?" Annie asked, faking confused surprise. She didn't want to appear *too* interested.

"To protect Lars's pet project." Shaking his head, Mr. Mack drummed his fingers on his desk.

What pet project? Annie's pulse rate jumped in alarm, but she kept her cool. Closing the office door, she sat on a chair in front of the desk. She understood her father's agitation. Although Lars was supposed to be working *with* him on GC-161, it was obvious that Danielle Atron favored the new man. And Lars never missed an opportunity to take advantage of it.

"Figures." Annie sighed in sympathy, then cautiously fished for more information. "But it must be something really important or the police wouldn't have cooperated."

"The Paradise Valley Police Department will do just about anything Danielle Atron wants. . . ."

Annie nodded. The whole town depended on the plant, including the local law enforcement agency. The CEO made generous contributions to the police benevolent fund every year.

"But to be fair—" Mr. Mack continued. "I suppose Lars's cryogenic experiments might have some commercial value eventually."

"Cryogenic experiments?"

Mr. Mack hastened to explain. "That's the study of how low temperatures—freezing temperatures to be specific—affect the properties of matter."

Annie knew what cryogenic studies were, but she let her father talk. She suspected the nature of the experiments was not common knowledge around the company. If she interrupted him, he might think twice about taking her into his confidence—not because he didn't trust her, but to protect her.

"Cryobiology is probably a more accurate definition, since Lars's project involves the effects of freezing temperatures on living organisms." Mr. Mack paused.

Annie prodded him. "What kind of organisms?"

"Plants." Mr. Mack leaned forward to peer at Annie intently. "I don't know the details, but he injected fifty full-grown, potted sunflowers with a variation of a substance he's been working on for years. Then he froze the plants in huge blocks of ice."

"And he hopes they'll still be alive and growing when he thaws them," Annie finished.

"Exactly." Mr. Mack sat back suddenly, then leaned forward again and spoke softly. "Except nobody without A-1 level clearance is supposed to know what's in those blocks of ice or why. Lars is convinced industrial spies from other companies have infiltrated PVCP."

"My lips are sealed," Annie whispered back. If Lars's experiment succeeded, the discovery would have invaluable agricultural applications. An advanced phase of the substance might make it possible to protect citrus groves from killing frosts. Florida growers would pay a high price for such a treatment. The possibilities were endless, Annie realized.

"The thing is," Mr. Mack went on, speaking more to himself than Annie, "I think Lars's *real* goal is a cryonic process that works on people."

"Freezing *people?*" This time Annie didn't have to act surprised. She really was.

"Freezing terminally ill or dead people," Mr. Mack corrected. "With the intent of bringing them back alive when cures for their diseases are found. It's an idea that's been around for a long time. Only nobody's been able to do it, yet."

Her father's theory made perfect sense to Annie. Lars *was* from Europe, where there was a lot of interest in such studies. The formula for his substance might be worth stealing. But that didn't answer the next question that came to her mind.

"What does that have to do with police roadblocks in Paradise Valley?"

"Ms. Atron asked the police department to clear the main routes so the refrigerated trucks wouldn't have to stop."

"Trucks?" Annie was just getting more confused.

Mr. Mack nodded. "Right. The alarm went off because an electrical malfunction shorted out the compressor in Fredrickson's freezer. The experiment will be a total loss if the sunflower ice blocks start to thaw. So Ms. Atron hired refrigerated trucks to take them to freezers in grocery stores all over town. Just until the plant compressor is fixed."

"Oh." Annie exhaled with relief. GC-161 hadn't been the cause of the alarm or Lars's panic.

Alex was safe.

Shocked by the unexpected sight of the Paradise Valley Chemical logo on the back of a blue shirt, Alex hesitated.

The cake box hovered in midair just out of reach.

Moving backward, the driver dragged a dolly loaded with a huge ice block through the flapping plastic strips.

Snapping back to her senses, Alex telekinetically yanked the cake box closer. She grabbed it with her hands just as the driver looked over his shoulder.

Dave!

"Hello." Dave touched the brim of his cap and smiled.

Clutching the cake box, Alex stared at him. Even though Danielle Atron had fired Vince and demoted Dave back to being a truck driver, Dave still made her nervous. He was always friendly when their paths chanced to cross, but he was also the only witness to the accident that had drenched her in GC-161. Getting fired seemed like a picnic compared to what would happen to her in Danielle Atron's lab. The CEO of the chemical plant wasn't actively looking for her anymore, but Ms. Atron wouldn't turn down the prize if Dave finally remembered and identified her as the GC-161 kid.

The storage freezer at the Plaza Market was the last place Alex had expected to run into him.

"Excuse me," Dave said as he turned the dolly.

"Sure." Alex pressed closer to the stacks of cardboard cartons to make room as Dave unloaded the ice block against the back wall. It looked like something was stuck in the middle of the cloudy block, but she couldn't tell what. She didn't know why Dave was delivering ice, either, and she didn't care. *Just as long as he isn't looking for me. . . .*

Dave glanced back as he pushed the empty dolly to the door. "You should be wearing a sweater in there. It's freezing."

"Let's go, Dave!" Lars Fredrickson paused on the far side of the plastic strips. His bald head gleamed and the goatee beard on his chin twitched as he flexed his jaw in agitation. "It's a good thing I sent my technicians with the other drivers and decided to supervise *you* personally."

"Coming, Mr. Fredrickson."

"Well, hurry up! I've got to check the other freezer drops before we go back to the plant—"

Alex jumped as the tall, thin chemist slammed the door closed.

CHAPTER 6

Alex wasn't afraid of being locked in. The freezer door had an interior handle to prevent anyone from getting trapped inside.

Her nerves were totally shot.

Aside from the surprise encounter with Dave, the couple of minutes it should have taken to stash the cake had stretched into ten. Skipping her fifteen-minute break would still pay back the time, but she felt bad about "goofing off" anyway.

After shoving the cake box into the space where the orange juice carton had been, Alex ran to the door and opened it. Moving as quietly as possible, she eased out of the freezer and scooted behind the pallets. Taking a deep breath, she pushed the cart full of rotted lemons into the open.

Dave was hauling another ice block out of the truck. Mrs. Argyle wasn't in sight, but Mr. Lindsey was talking with Lars on the loading dock.

"I know it's inconvenient, Mr. Lindsey, but the freezer must *not* be opened again until after we remove the ice."

"And when will that be?" Mr. Lindsey did not sound happy.

"As soon as the plant compressor is fixed and our freezer reaches the proper temperature," Lars explained. "This is an important experiment and Ms. Atron *really* appreciates your cooperation."

Mr. Lindsey nodded. "I'll be glad to help out any way I can."

"Well, I'm glad to hear that," Lars said. "You'll have to lower the temperature in your freezer, too."

Mr. Lindsey sighed. "Of course. Whatever you want."

A wise decision, Alex thought as she reached the dumpster and lifted the lemon crate out of the cart. Not cooperating with Danielle Atron would be a majorly stupid thing to do.

"There you are, Alex!"

Alex braced herself as Mrs. Argyle scurried across the storeroom. Taking an early break was one thing, but if Mrs. Argyle asked where she had been, she couldn't lie.

Luckily, the produce manager didn't seem to know or care about her short disappearance. Mrs. Argyle had lemons on her mind.

"Oh, my." The woman gently slapped her hand to her face as she looked into the crate. "Harvey said you had found some bad lemons, but I had no idea it was so many. I wonder how much other rotted stuff is out there. . . ."

Alex shrugged. "I don't know, but I'll trash whatever I find."

"I'm sure you will, but it'll have to wait until tomorrow. The Friday afternoon rush is starting and they need you at the checkout."

"On my way." Dumping the lemons, Alex grabbed the cart and raced for the front of the store. Somehow she had managed to avert one catastrophe after another all day, but the stress of so many close calls was wearing her down.

Convinced that things would be better tomorrow, Alex glanced at the clock high on the front wall. It was five minutes to three. Her shift ended at six.

Only three hours to go and she'd be home free.

Alex lined up the "out" space with the arrow on the face of the time clock, then pushed the card into the horizontal slot. A printing mechanism inside punched the time with a sharp *ka-chunk!* Alex sighed with relief as she removed the card and glanced at the imprint.

6:03 P.M.

Made it!

Slipping the card into a narrow, metal rack attached to the wall by the emergency exit, Alex pulled off the ponytail holder and shook out her long, blond hair. She had spent the past three hours bagging groceries and helping customers carry them to their cars. She was bone-tired and her feet hurt, but she hadn't dropped, squashed, or broken anything. Mr. Lindsey and Mrs. Argyle had both complimented her enthusiasm and eagerness to learn and expected her to do fine in spite of her rocky start.

And they don't know just how rocky it really was, Alex thought with a grin. But the invisible specter of disaster seemed to have given up its campaign to get her fired, and she was actually looking forward to coming back to the store tomorrow morning.

Preoccupied with getting home to change for the rally, Alex almost left through the emergency exit. She pulled her hand off the bar-handle an instant before she pressed down. The electronic lock was disengaged during business hours, but an alarm was set to go off when the door was opened by anyone going in or out. Mr. Lindsey would not have appreciated *that* during the Friday night rush!

Shaking her head, Alex dashed back across the empty employee break room and through a door that opened into the storeroom beside Mrs. Argyle's office. She remembered her mother's cake the moment she saw the freezer. Pressed for time and pressing her luck, Alex hurried to the freezer. She opened the door, parted the plastic strips and gasped.

When she had stashed the cake, the middle section of the large compartment had been empty. Now, the entire freezer was crammed from side to side to within a foot of the door with the huge ice blocks from the plant. There was no room to get by them and they were too tall to climb over.

Alex threw up her hands in frustration. The cake was in the back and there was only one way she was going to reach it.

Glancing over her shoulder to make sure she was alone, Alex morphed. A tingling warmth flooded her as the cells in her body transformed from solid to liquid. Dissolving into a puddle of ooze, she slid through the plastic strips.

The cold in the freezer was far more intense than anything Alex had experienced before. Recently, she had discovered that cold temperatures had a definite physical effect when she was liquified. She could stay morphed longer, but she couldn't move as fast.

Alex paused at the base of the massive ice blocks to plot her course. Going up the face of the ice and over the top was the most direct route to the white box hidden on top of the cartons in the corner. With no time to waste, she began to glide up the front of the ice. An uncontrollable attack of shivers hit before she had gone halfway. When she finally oozed over the top edge, the shivering stopped as a numbing cold seeped into her liquid cells. Slowed down by the frigid cold, she was barely inching over the surface of the ice.

I feel like an arctic slug, Alex thought miserably. *I don't have time for this!* Then she had a brainstorm. Now that she was on top of the tall blocks, she could finish the job as her solid self. She had to materialize to pick up the cake, anyway, and she could move faster as a person. Lowering herself down from the ice blocks did not present the same problem as trying to climb up, either. Gravity would be on her side.

Alex visualized herself lying down as she mentally set the transformation process in motion. There wasn't enough room between the top of the ice blocks and the ceiling to morph back standing up. More seconds than usual passed before the warm tingles triggered her liquid cells to shift to solid form. Alex felt a moment's apprehension, but it was instantly forgotten as she materialized stretched out on the freezing bed of ice.

Scrambling to her knees, Alex quickly crawled across the ice blocks to the end of the freezer. The white cake box was sitting in the niche right where she left it. Tucking the box under one arm, she started back to the door on her knees. She was shivering again and it seemed much colder in the freezer than it had earlier. It *was* colder, Alex realized, remembering Lars's conversation with Mr. Lindsey. The plant chemist had asked the store manager to lower the temperature for the ice blocks.

Alex hesitated on the block closest to the door. She had been so focused on her own problems, she hadn't been the least bit curious about why Danielle Atron's star scientist was so worried about a bunch of giant ice cubes. Obviously, they weren't just ordinary ice blocks. Peering down, Alex could just make out the dark brown, yellow-petal-fringed circle of a huge sunflower staring back.

Alex blinked at the sight of the forlorn, frozen plant. Why would anyone want to freeze sunflowers?

"Who opened the freezer?" Mr. Lindsey's angry voice rang through the storeroom. "And left it open!"

Alex inhaled sharply. She could just make out Mr. Lindsey storming toward the freezer through the breaks in the plastic strips. She had forgotten that Lars had told the store manager to keep the door closed.

She was trapped with no place to hide.

Not as a flesh-and-blood person, anyway.

But the ice block would provide perfect camouflage if she was a puddle of silvery ooze.

Tightening her grip on the ice cream cake, Alex morphed.

Since she had been exposed to the supercold temperatures in the freezer for several minutes, the process was agonizingly slow. Alex had just finished transforming and flattening herself on the ice when Mr. Lindsey stepped into the open doorway and parted the plastic strips. Upset and scowling, he scanned the ice-packed interior.

To Alex, the passing seconds felt like an eternity. Shivers rippled over her fluid form, then subsided as the bitter-cold numbness settled in again.

Then Mr. Lindsey realized he was just making the situation worse by standing there with the door open. He backed up and slammed it closed, shutting off the light.

Another narrow escape, Alex thought as total darkness engulfed her.

And now she was going to be even later getting to the rally. She knew Nicole would understand that she had run into some unavoidable delays, but she didn't like going back on a promise—not even when she had a good excuse.

So stop thinking about it and get moving, Alex!

Since she was already morphed, Alex felt her way over the edge of the block and oozed down the wall of ice. Even with gravity helping, she still seemed to be moving sluggishly slow. However, as she pooled into a puddle on the floor, the cold didn't seem so bad. Maybe because her liquid cells had adjusted to it.

The closed freezer door was airtight and Alex couldn't get out while she was still morphed, but she was sure the space between the door and the front of the stacked ice was big enough for her slim body. Once she was solid again, she could just turn the handle and walk out . . . and hope Mr. Lindsey wasn't hanging around, waiting to catch the person who left the freezer door open.

He doesn't have to worry, though, Alex thought as she positioned herself in the middle of the space. The brutal cold that had penetrated her liquid cells was proof that the temperature in the freezer had not risen a fraction of a degree despite the open door. The ice blocks had *not* started to thaw.

Alex filled her mind with an image of her real self, engaging the morph sequence.

Except for the first few times she had tried right after the GC-161 chemical altered her genetic makeup, morphing back and forth between solid and liquid had become second nature to Alex. When she decided to change into a puddle, she did—instantly. When she decided to change back into a girl, she did that instantly, too. The shift was never a problem.

Until now.

As her liquid self elongated into a tall glob, Alex realized that something was wrong. Usually, the warm tingling sensation that flowed through her as she ballooned to full-size intensified. Then a hot flash radiated through her a split second before she was solid again.

The warm tingling wasn't getting warmer. It was cooling down.

Concentrating all her energies, Alex desperately tried to complete the transformation to solid form.

She just got colder and colder.

Finally, Alex had to accept a terrifying truth.

She was solid again, all right.

Frozen solid!

CHAPTER 7

Alex had never felt so helpless in her whole life.

Still morphed, she had frozen before she could change back into her real self!

Alex had found herself in several frightening situations because something had affected her powers over the past couple of years. Like when she caught Ray's cold and all her powers had gone berserk while a reporter who was spying for the plant was in the house. Or when she got trapped in the dryer and a chemical from an antistatic sheet got into her system so she couldn't control her morphing. Then there was the time Vince had treated the carnival tickets with some anti-GC-161 stuff that turned her into a walking magnet.

But all those incidents seemed like minor inconveniences compared to this!

She had turned into a giant icicle that couldn't move or talk. However, the whirring sound of the freezer compressor was muffled, but audible. She couldn't see, either, but she suspected that wasn't because her vision wasn't working. The freezer was totally dark. But beyond that, she couldn't do anything but stand there and worry.

And she had a *lot* to worry about. As if being frozen wasn't bad enough, she was frozen with a bunch of sunflowers encased in huge ice blocks that were some kind of important experiment at Paradise Valley Chemical. What if she got hauled back to the plant with the rest of the ice? And even more unsettling—what did Lars plan to do with the massive ice blocks when he got them back?

Alex's mind reeled as she considered the possible consequences of her predicament.

The European chemist hadn't shown any interest in the kid who had been doused with GC-161. But that would sure change in a hurry if she thawed into a puddle and materialized back into a girl right in front of him!

Alex decided not to think about it. Dwelling on a worst-case scenario wasn't serving any purpose but to scare her more than she already was.

Think positive, Alex! There has to be something good about being frozen.

There was one thing, Alex realized. She didn't feel the cold anymore. Her cells had adjusted to this new state-of-being as easily as they adapted to anything when she morphed. And she was pretty sure she'd defrost and be okay as soon as she was exposed to warmer temperatures. Annie would know. In fact, Annie would be fascinated.

I should probably take mental notes.

Actually, that wasn't a bad idea, Alex realized. She had no doubt that Annie would want to know every little detail concerning the accidental freezing experiment. And it would give her something constructive to do—

Annie!

Alex felt her first glimmer of hope. Annie always came to her rescue. No matter how bizarre her power-related problems were or how impossible solutions to those problems seemed to be, Annie never failed to come through.

When Annie knew there was a problem. . . .
But *that* wasn't a problem, either.

It wouldn't be long before Annie started wondering why Alex hadn't shown up from work to change for the rally. Not that her sister cared about her social life or her appearance. Annie would be upset and angry if she thought Alex had forgotten to bring home the ice cream cake.

The minute Annie looked in the refrigerator freezer and realized the Brewster's Sweet Shoppe box wasn't there, she'd start looking for her.

Alex was sure of it.

Annie and Mr. Mack were just getting out of the car when Mrs. Mack pulled into the driveway behind them.

"Perfect timing!" Mrs. Mack jumped out of her car and waved. "You've got ten minutes to change, George!"

"Change?" Puzzled, Mr. Mack glanced at Annie.

Annie shrugged. She wasn't going to spoil her mom's surprise. She had spent the past hour desperately trying to rush her father home without saying anything about the dinner reservations. However, no amount of urging had deterred him from his errands. They had stood in line for twenty minutes at the bank waiting to deposit his paycheck. Then he had stopped to fill the car with gas, check the oil, and run it through the automatic car wash.

"Dinner, dear." Mrs. Mack hurried over with her arms full of books. "I thought we could use a night out—just the two of us. We've got seven o'clock reservations at the Blue Moon."

Mr. Mack grinned, surprised and pleased. "Great, but we'd better get going. It's six-thirty now." He led Annie and Mrs. Mack up the front walk, then stopped short at the door with a stricken look.

"What's the matter, George? Aren't you in the mood for Chinese?"

"No, I mean—yes. The Blue Moon is my favorite restaurant, but—" Sighing, Mr. Mack pulled a beeper out of his pocket. "I'm on emergency call."

Mrs. Mack raised an eyebrow. "At a chemical plant?"

"We had an equipment breakdown today," Mr. Mack explained as he followed Mrs. Mack inside. "It's a top secret project, so everyone with high-level security clearance is expected to help if maintenance gets the problem fixed tonight."

Annie exchanged guarded looks with her father, but didn't say anything. As far as everyone else was concerned, she didn't know anything about the cryobiology experiment.

"Well, no matter." Mrs. Mack smiled, refusing to let something that might not happen dampen her spirits. "We've got to eat, anyway, so let's just go. If your beeper goes off during dinner, I'll bring the leftovers home for later."

As Mr. Mack ran upstairs to change into more casual clothes, Mrs. Mack dropped her books on the couch, then drew Annie aside. "Did you get the cake?"

"Yes, but I had to give it to Alex because I was running late. But don't worry. She put it in the freezer at the market."

"Okay." Mrs. Mack glanced at her watch. "What time does she get off?"

"Six."

"Then she should be home by now." Mrs. Mack frowned thoughtfully, then called up the stairs. "Alex!"

There was no answer.

"She's probably already been here and gone,

Mom. She said something about changing for the basketball game rally. Her class is selling sodas to raise money for charity."

Reassured, Mrs. Mack glanced down at her own campus attire. "Speaking of changing, I think I'll get out of these jeans and into something a little more—"

"Alluring?" Annie suggested mischievously.

"Grown-up."

The minute her mother disappeared into the bedroom, Annie headed for the kitchen to check the freezer. It wasn't that she didn't trust Alex to keep her word, but her sister didn't have the most organized mind in the world. If Alex was worried about changing and getting to the rally on time, she might have forgotten all about the cake.

The phone rang, then rang a second time.

"I'll get it." Annie picked up on her way past the counter. "Hello."

"Hi, Annie. It's Ray. Is Alex there?"

"No. I think she's on her way to the rally." Annie opened the freezer. *No cake. Wonderful.*

"Oh. I was hoping to catch her before she left. When we stopped to pick up the sodas at the store, she told us she'd be late."

"She did?" Closing the freezer, Annie leaned against the counter. "What time was that, Ray?"

"Around quarter to three."

After I dropped the cake off, Annie thought. It *was* Friday. A lot of people cashed their paychecks and went grocery shopping after work. Maybe the store had asked Alex to stay through the rush. If she hadn't gotten home yet, that would explain why the ice cream cake wasn't there, either.

"I don't suppose I could talk you into doing us a really big favor," Ray asked cautiously.

"Like what?" Annie asked back, matching his caution.

"Can we borrow your cooler? And would you drive it over?" Ray sounded slightly frantic. "Katy Robertson was supposed to bring one, but she got sick and I've got two bags of ice melting all over the place."

Annie paused thoughtfully. She didn't have any definite plans for tonight. Everyone was going to the rally and the big game. It was also possible that Alex *was* walking to the school and just hadn't arrived. Which would mean she *had* forgotten to bring the cake home. There was only one way to find out. Drive the route and look for her.

"Sure, Ray. No problem."

"Thanks, Annie. I owe you one."

Mr. and Mrs. Mack were just going out the door when Annie intercepted them.

"Were there any messages?" Annie glanced upstairs, indicating the answering machine in her parents' room.

"No," Mrs. Mack said. "Guess we're not very popular today."

Alex hadn't called. But, Annie realized, if the store was really busy, she might not have had a chance to use the phone. And if she was headed for the rally, Alex didn't have a reason to call. Annie considered calling the store, then changed her mind. Employees weren't allowed to accept personal phone calls unless there was an emergency—and an ice cream cake just didn't qualify.

"Can I use Mom's car to go to the school? Ray wants to borrow the cooler."

Mr. Mack nodded. "Just don't be too late."

"We'll be back around nine," Mrs. Mack said, winking at her older daughter as she urged her husband out the door.

"Unless I get called back to the plant," Mr.

Mack mumbled. "Then who knows what time I'll get home!"

When they had gone, Annie got the cooler from the garage and tossed it into the backseat of the car. If Alex was at the rally, she'd just have to leave to go back to the store for the cake. If Alex wasn't at the rally, then she *and* the cake were still at the store. *No problem either way*, Annie thought. As long as the cake was in the freezer when her parents got home in two hours, everything would be fine.

She had plenty of time.

CHAPTER 8

Alex had no idea how long she had been frozen and stuck in the Plaza Market freezer. Her sense of time was totally distorted.

Being frozen was boring!

Taking mental notes had kept her occupied for a while. Alex had repeatedly reviewed the freak series of events that had turned her into a popsicle and committed the cause-and-effect details to memory. But then her thoughts had focused right back on Paradise Valley Chemical and Lars Fredrickson's frozen sunflowers. If the plant came back for the ice blocks before Annie found her, she would become part of the experiment.

And there's nothing I can do about it!

Alex balked at the idea of surrendering without a fight. She had managed to avoid becoming one of the plant's experiments for more than two years. She was not going to spoil a perfect record and become a PVCP laboratory subject now. Somehow, she had to get out of this mess.

What's taking Annie so long?

Alex was absolutely positive that her sister would find her. The ice cream cake was the clue that would lead her to the storeroom freezer in the grocery store. She had hidden it in the huge storage freezer at *Annie's* suggestion. And no way would Annie take "no" for an answer when she asked someone to check the freezer. And Annie wouldn't rely on someone else's search, either. Her stubborn, meticulous older sister would want to see for herself if the ice cream cake was still there—

The cake isn't *here!* Alex realized suddenly. *It's morphed and frozen, too! And what if Annie doesn't figure out that the block of ice in front is me?*

Alex refused to panic. Losing control to her fears and frustrations wouldn't solve anything. She had to *do* something!

Alex had never really tried using her other

powers when she was liquified. Circumstances had never made it necessary and only being able to stay morphed for five minutes did not give her much time to experiment.

Time was one thing she had plenty of now. She might as well put it to good use.

Annie would certainly notice if a miniature lightning bolt suddenly flashed through one of the ice blocks. But trying to zap probably wasn't a good idea, Alex decided. Even if she managed to discharge a little electrical energy, she didn't have fingers to direct it. She couldn't be sure, but a random burst of electricity throughout her frozen self might have disastrous results. She could end up with permanently frizzy hair or she might short out some vitally necessary part of herself or the freezer. Annie would know, but Annie wasn't there to consult.

So zapping was not an option. And even if she could see through the metal door, that wouldn't attract her sister's attention. On the other hand, telekinesis presented some intriguing possibilities.

Alex stared into the darkness in front of her and telekinetically groped for the door handle. When she found it, she tried to turn it—with no results. The handle had to be yanked down with a lot of *physical* force to release the catch. Apparently, her telekinetic power was not nearly as effective when she was frozen. But she wasn't going to let that discourage her.

Alex mentally reached for the top carton stacked to the left. The box was too heavy to move and she switched to the top carton on the right. Concentrating, she focused all the telekinetic energy she could muster.

The box rocked slightly and then she lost it. However, she thought the rocking motion had shifted the carton forward a little.

Not much, Alex thought with elation. But if she kept at it, she could eventually jiggle it over the edge and off the box underneath it. It would take a while, but she didn't have anything better to do.

Alex went to work. Everything was going to be fine—as long as Annie didn't get there *too* soon.

Alex wasn't at the rally or on any of the streets Annie had driven up and down searching for her.

"She'll be here, Annie," Ray insisted as he

poured two bags of watery ice into the cooler. "If she wasn't going to show up, she would have told someone."

"I know. That's why I'm starting to worry." Annie frowned. What if something had happened to Alex on her way home? She had been so worried about the cake, she hadn't considered that possibility before. Now, the cake didn't seem quite so important.

"Alex *did* say she was going to be late," Nicole added. "Although I didn't expect her to be *this* late. It's seven-fifteen already."

"And we're almost out of sodas," Robyn said.

"Great. As soon as we're sold out, we can go join in the fun." Louis ripped the plastic wrapper off the last case of mixed flavors and began shoving the cans into the ice-filled cooler. "Although we might have trouble selling these. They're warm."

A girl ran up to the table and handed Nicole three quarters. She picked out a can of warm soda, shrugged, and ran back to join the squad.

"Not a problem, Louis. We've got the only sodas on the field and those guys are working up a thirst." Nicole put the coins in the cashbox and nodded toward the cheering crowd gathered around the outside basketball court. The cheer-leaders were jumping up and down on the side-lines while the varsity basketball team warmed up on the court. "We'll be sold out in fifteen minutes. Tops."

Annie studied the crowd, then scanned the parking lot and sidewalks. There was still no sign of Alex.

"Yeah, but our team is going to wear them-selves out showing off before the game even gets started." Ray shook his head. "I won't do that when I'm on the varsity squad."

"Come on, Ray." Louis picked up the soda carton and plastic. "Help me dump the trash. I want to get a good seat in the gym before this crowd decides it's time to go inside for the game."

Annie touched Ray's arm as he snapped open a trash bag. "I'm gonna leave the cooler with you, Ray. I've got to go look for Alex."

Ray hesitated. "It *is* getting kind of late, isn't it?"

Annie nodded. "She's probably home or at the store or somewhere between here and there, but I'm not gonna be able to relax until I *know* Alex is okay."

"Me, neither. Give me five minutes and I'll go with you. Nicole will take care of the cooler."

"Five minutes, Ray, then I'm out of here."

It was seven-thirty when Annie and Ray drove out of the school parking lot. After cruising every possible route Alex might have taken between home and the school, they pulled into the Macks' driveway. The house seemed like the logical place to look next. But Alex wasn't there, and Annie was certain she hadn't been there. The cake was not in the freezer and her work clothes were not tossed in a heap on their bedroom floor. There were no messages on the machine, either. It was almost eight when they reached the Plaza Market parking lot.

Annie glanced at two baggers helping customers load their groceries into cars as she followed Ray to the entrance. Alex wasn't one of them. Once they were inside, it took only a few seconds to scan the checkout counters.

"She's not here," Ray said, his worried frown deepening.

"It doesn't look too busy. Maybe she just got off," Annie said hopefully. But she didn't really believe it. Alex was two hours overdue. Rush or no rush, when Alex realized that she was going to be more than a half hour late, she would have convinced her boss to let her call home so her family wouldn't worry.

"Looks like Mr. Lindsey's working late, too." Ray pointed to a tall man behind the customer service desk. "Let's ask him. He's the manager."

"No, wait a minute." Annie hesitated, remembering that Alex was worried about store policy and storing the cake. She didn't want to jeopardize Alex's job, especially if it wasn't necessary. "We'll save him as a last resort. Maybe one of these other kids has seen her."

A heavyset girl on checkout number seven started for the back of the store.

"Excuse me!" Annie called as she and Ray followed the girl down the cereal aisle.

The girl paused. "Can I help you?"

"Do you know if Alex Mack is still working?"

"Or when she left?" Ray added.

"Alex Mack?" The girl shook her head. "Sorry. I don't know any Alex M—"

"I know her," a voice said from behind them. "She left a while ago."

The girl moved on as Annie and Ray turned to face a boy returning a box of cereal to the shelves.

"Are you sure"—Annie glanced at the name badge on his shirt—"Harvey?"

"Yeah, pretty sure. But it's been so busy, I haven't paid much attention to anything except plastic bags and groceries."

"How long ago did she leave?" Ray asked.

Harvey shrugged. "I could check the time clock to see when she punched out."

"That would help," Annie said.

Tight-lipped and tense, Annie and Ray didn't stop following him when Harvey walked through swinging double doors marked Employees Only and into a large storeroom. Harvey glanced back, hesitated uncertainly, but then continued on. He turned right and went through a smaller door into an employee break room. The time clock was on a wall by an emergency exit.

Nervous and impatient, Annie glanced from the door to the time clock to the rack as Harvey slowly flipped through the cards. He finally pulled one out.

"She clocked out at three minutes after six."

"So where is she?" Ray asked anxiously.

Annie shook her head as she tried to figure out what to do next.

Harvey's eyes widened. "Gosh, I hope nothing's happened to her."

"Yeah." Exhaling, Annie ran her hand through her dark hair. "Actually, there is something else you could do that might give us a clue, Harvey."

"Anything," Harvey said sincerely.

"Thanks. Would you check the freezer in the storeroom for a white cake box from Brewster's Sweet Shoppe?"

"I can't." Harvey paled. "That guy from the chemical plant said nobody could open the freezer until they picked up those big blocks of ice. If Mr. Lindsey finds out, I could lose my job."

Annie understood the boy's reluctance and she was certain Alex hadn't tangled with anyone from the plant. The ice had been dropped off around three and Alex had been fine when she clocked out at six. But Annie had to know about the cake before she could plan her next move. The cake was the clue to Alex's actions after six.

Annie tapped the time card in Harvey's hand. "Nobody's heard from Alex since she punched out. Please . . ."

*　　*　　*

Another interesting effect of being frozen, Alex noted as she took a telekinetic break, *is that I'm not tired. But I can't generate much energy, either.* Moving the carton had taken a lot of time and effort. However, if her calculations were right, she only had to jiggle it forward another half inch or so, and then she'd be able to topple it with a little telekinetic nudge. . . .

The sound of the door handle turning would have frozen Alex in her tracks if she wasn't already frozen. Either the plant drivers had come back for their ice blocks or Annie had finally traced her back to the freezer.

But I'm not ready for Annie, Alex thought desperately. She needed a few more minutes to get the carton into position so she could topple it. Otherwise, Annie wouldn't notice her.

The door cracked open.

The plant or Annie?

Either way, she was out of luck.

CHAPTER 9

The overhead light flashed on.

Alex immediately turned her attention from the door to the carton and read the black printed words on the end.

Frozen waffles.

That explained why the box was so light. Since she had just taken a break, she might be able to pull the box off the stack if she really concentrated. She had worked too hard to give up now—

But what if it isn't Annie?

The crucial question made Alex pause. She waited, poised to spring into telekinetic action depending on who was on the other side of the door.

The heavy metal barrier swung wide.

Harvey pushed the plastic strips aside.

And Alex saw Annie and Ray scurrying across the storeroom behind him.

Harvey looked over his shoulder and waved them to stay back.

Alex took the opportunity to hit the carton with a barrage of short telekinetic tugs. The box jolted forward with a scraping sound.

Harvey jumped.

Alex stopped a split second before he looked back into the freezer with a nervous, puzzled expression.

The waffle carton teetered on the verge of falling.

Warned off by Harvey, Annie and Ray paused by the stack of pallets Alex had used for cover that afternoon. Both of them stretched to see into the freezer. Alex wasn't sure, but since she had frozen right before materializing, she probably looked lumpy compared to the other rectangular ice blocks. Annie was bound to notice the difference.

Except Harvey was blocking Annie's view!

Harvey's gaze quickly swept the inside of the freezer. "There's no cake box in here." He jumped back, as though he couldn't wait to close the door and get out of there.

Alex yanked on the waffle box with all her mental might. The carton lifted off the box underneath and wobbled above it.

"Are you sure?" Annie asked, stepping to the side to look around him.

"Positive," Harvey said sharply.

Alex lost her telekinetic grip and the waffle box fell to the floor.

Annie raised her arm just as the door slammed closed.

Was Annie trying to signal her?

Waiting and wondering, Alex counted off the seconds.

The door did not open again.

Ray didn't argue when Harvey hurried over and began to herd them toward the double doors.

"Sorry, but you guys have to get out of here before Mr. Lindsey finds you and blames me for letting you into an unauthorized area."

Annie wasn't ready to leave. "But—"

"You're not supposed to be in here, and I really need this job," Harvey pleaded.

"Come on, Annie. He's right." Ray nodded grimly and started walking. Even though the cake was gone and Alex was nowhere to be found, Harvey had taken enough risks trying to help them. Annie took the hint and followed.

Harvey opened one of the doors, looked around, then stepped back. "It's safe. Nobody's out there."

Ray pushed the door open and let Annie go through first. He stopped once he was on the other side and held out his hand. "Thanks, Harve. It was totally cool of you to put your job on the line like that."

Harvey sighed as he shook Ray's hand. "Yeah, not that it did any good."

"It did a lot of good, Harvey," Annie said graciously. "We'll find her."

"Right," Ray said with less conviction than he felt. He was sure Annie was just trying to keep Harvey from worrying, too. "At least, now we know where she's not."

"I suppose. Call me—one way or the other, okay? I'll be here until we close at ten."

"You got it." Ray gave the boy a thumbs-up as Annie tugged on his sleeve to get him moving.

Back outside, Annie ran to the car and jumped in. She had the engine started before Ray finished fastening his seatbelt.

"Now what?" Ray asked despondently. Alex seemed to have vanished into thin air and he didn't have a clue what to do next.

Annie was too intent on driving to answer. The instant he closed the door, she backed out of the parking space and headed in the wrong direction.

"We have to go the other way to get out of the parking lot, Annie. There's no drive at this end."

"I know."

"Uh-huh." Ray sat back and frowned as Annie turned left around the corner of the grocery store.

A large furniture store on the right formed a high, windowless wall that ran the entire length of the narrow driveway. Annie cruised slowly past the emergency exit from the employee break room and the raised loading docks. She peered out the side window without saying a word.

"What are we doing?" Ray asked finally.

"Casing the joint."

Ray blinked, then decided Annie had taken refuge in humor because she was worried sick about her missing sister. But they didn't have time for jokes.

"Shouldn't we be looking for Alex? She could be in major trouble, Annie. I mean, what if Vince finally saw her using her powers and kidnapped her or something?"

Ray shuddered at the thought he had been avoiding since Alex failed to show up at the rally. Danielle Atron had fired Vince because he hadn't found the GC-161 kid, but that hadn't stopped him from looking. The ex-CIA agent, ex-head of security at PVCP was more determined than ever. Identifying Alex was Vince's only chance to salvage his damaged reputation and soothe his wounded pride.

"Vince doesn't have Alex, Ray." Speeding up slightly, Annie drove around the back of the building.

"You can't be sure of that—" Ray looked at Annie askance. "Not unless you know something I don't. Did she find out she can become invisible or what?"

"Hardly. She's in the freezer, Ray."

"No, she's not. There's nothing in that freezer

but cardboard boxes and a bunch of big ice blocks. Your mom's ice cream cake isn't there, either."

"Wrong. Alex has it and Alex is one of the blocks." Annie sighed as she finished circling the store and drove down the drive. "Don't ask me why or how, but Alex morphed in the freezer and froze before she could morph back."

"Are you sure?"

"Yes, absolutely." Annie turned right onto the street, heading back toward their neighborhood. "I was suspicious when I noticed that lumpy block of ice in the front. It's exactly the same size and shape Alex is before she morphs back into herself. But when that box lifted off the shelf right before Harvey closed the door, I knew. That falling box was a signal, Ray. From Alex. I don't know if she saw me wave or not."

Ray was stunned. Annie's theory made a weird kind of sense, but it also presented another urgent problem. "Will being frozen hurt her?"

"Hard to say. She's obviously alert and thinking clearly and I know she can see because she moved the box when Harvey wasn't looking. Her telekinetic power works, too. So chances are she'll be all right." Annie scowled thoughtfully.

"Hopefully, her morphed cellular structure is more adaptable than normal cells."

"Hopefully?" Ray's throat constricted with dread. "What happens to regular cells?"

"The water in them freezes, and freezing water expands, which ruptures the cell membrane."

"Oh, well, that's just great."

"I honestly don't think she'll have any cell damage." Annie caught Ray's eye with a quick, sidelong glance. "As long as she thaws naturally."

"We have to do something, Annie. We can't just leave her there."

"I know, but we can't just walk in and get her, either."

"Why not?" Ray grinned. "We'll go ask for a huge block of ice and buy her!"

"I wish it was that simple, but it's not. That ice belongs to the plant."

"The plant!" Ray sagged as Annie explained about the broken PVCP freezer and Lars's experiment.

"So there's only one thing we can do," Annie finished.

"I'm afraid to ask." Ray hesitated a moment, then asked, "What?"

Annie stopped at a traffic light and looked him square in the eye. "We've got to break into the store after it closes and steal her."

"I knew I shouldn't have asked."

But Ray also knew they didn't have any choice.

CHAPTER 10

After changing into dark clothes, Annie had spent an hour searching the house and garage for anything that might help open the emergency exit door. Now, a nervous calm settled over her as she surveyed the array of equipment strewn across the kitchen table.

The battery on her notepad computer was fully charged and she had collected an assortment of alligator-clip wires, miniature probes, and other electronic gadgets that might come in handy. Properly connected and programmed, the computer could isolate the code sequence and key the electronic lock. She hoped. She also hoped one of the small, computer repair tools was the right size and shape to unlock the dead bolt. She also had wire cutters in case the alarm was electrical and not electronic.

Breathing in deeply, Annie began stuffing the tools in a black canvas bag. Alex had gotten herself into a lot of strange and dangerous situations in the past. Many of them had required a measure of risk and creative thinking on Annie's part to save her. Creative breaking-and-entering was another thing entirely.

A knot tightened in Annie's stomach. If she and Ray got caught, the consequences would be serious. They couldn't explain to the police that they were only trying to rescue her sister, the ice cube. They'd be arrested and Alex would end up at the plant. Maybe forever.

Annie was sure Lars's ultimate goal was to freeze people so they could be revived at a later time. If Alex began to thaw in the chemist's lab, it wouldn't take him long to realize that she was not just another block of ice. He'd find out that she had GC-161 in her system, which caused her to morph, and that morphed people could be frozen and thawed without harm. Alex would become a permanent test subject at PVCP because she represented a new, totally radical, but potentially successful approach to cryonic preservation that neither Lars nor Danielle Atron would be able to resist.

Assuming the freezing process worked, Annie reminded herself. She wouldn't know that until she got Alex back.

And she had to get her back no matter the risk. *I'm the one who gave her the cake to store when I should have brought it home. It's my fault she's in this mess.*

Slinging the bag of tools over her shoulder, Annie pocketed her driver's license, picked up the car keys, and glanced at the clock. Eight minutes after ten. She headed for the front door.

Mrs. Mack walked in just as Annie was about to turn the knob.

"Mom!" Annie hesitated. She had been so involved with Alex's problem, she had forgotten all about her mother's plans. The dessert was hardly important under the circumstances, but her mother didn't know that.

"Hi, Annie." Mrs. Mack dropped her purse on the hall table and looked at her daughter's black clothes and bag. "Are you going out again?"

"Uh—yeah. I'm—going to pick up Alex," Annie said. It *was* an honest answer.

Mrs. Mack nodded. "Why didn't you stay at the school? This was the deciding game for the play-offs, wasn't it?"

"I had some things to do. Where's Dad?"

Mrs. Mack sighed. "We were talking over coffee and his beeper went off. He dropped me off and went back to the plant."

Annie's mind lurched. If the plant freezer was fixed, the trucks might already be at the store to pick up the ice blocks!

"I don't think he'll get home until late," Mrs. Mack continued, "so we'll have to put off having the cake until tomorrow."

"That's okay." *One less thing to worry about*, Annie thought. Although she suspected the ice cream cake would be ice cream soup by the time Alex finished thawing out.

"Sorry." Shrugging apologetically, Mrs. Mack headed upstairs. "I'm going to bed. See you in the morning."

"Okay, Mom." Annie left, locking the door behind her.

Ray dashed across the lawn carrying his own

black bag. He had changed into black clothes, too.

"Hurry, Ray." Annie jumped into the driver's seat as Ray slipped in the passenger side. "We've got a problem."

"I'll say!" Ray rolled his eyes. "Your sister's frozen and we're about to become notorious neighborhood cat burglars."

"Worse," Annie said as she sped backward out of the driveway. "The freezer at the chemical plant is fixed."

"Step on it." Ray fastened his seat belt and clutched the black bag on his lap.

During the ten-minute drive back to the store, Annie explained how she hoped to get inside.

"When you said tools, I thought you meant *tools*." Ray peered inside his bag as Annie turned into the Plaza Market parking lot. "So I brought a hammer, pliers, wrenches—"

"Good. We might need them."

Annie stopped when she reached the far corner of the dark, deserted market. Security lights blazed over the emergency exit and the loading dock doors, but the plant trucks weren't there, yet. She backed into a parking space by the front corner of the store so the car wouldn't be blocking the narrow drive. She didn't have a clue what they would do if the plant trucks arrived before they finished their mission, then decided not to worry about that until it happened—if it happened.

Grabbing their bags, Annie and Ray slid out of the car and crouched. Both of them scanned the area. The grocery store was set well back from the street, so the car was not visible to passing traffic. The furniture store on the right was closed and dark, too. The only light in the driveway came from the grocery store security lamps.

Motioning for Ray to follow, Annie darted around the corner of the building and stopped just ouside the circle of light by the emergency door.

"We've got to get rid of that light," Ray hissed.

"I know, I know. . . ." Annie dropped her canvas bag and nervously searched the contents.

"What are you doing?" Ray asked.

"Looking for something to turn out the light. . . ."

"Consider it done."

Before Annie could protest, Ray smashed the light fixture with the hammer. Annie tensed as the sound of splintering glass ripped through the quiet night.

"There. It's turned off."

"It's also vandalism," Annie said angrily. "That's a crime!" Fortunately, she realized, looking around, no one seemed curious enough about the noise to investigate.

"So is breaking-and-entering," Ray said indignantly. "But if we're gonna get Alex out of there before the plant does, we don't have time to fool around."

Annie nodded. Ray had a valid point. They weren't trying to pull off a prank for kicks. Alex's life was in danger. And that made all the difference.

"Sorry, Ray." Annie pulled out the packet of computer tools and handed it to him. "You work on the dead bolt while I connect the computer to the electronic lock."

"I'm on it." Ray dropped to his knees before the door to give Annie room to work.

After plugging a lead into the notepad, Annie pushed a miniature probe into a small port beside a red LED in the lock. Although she hadn't been paying close attention when she was in the break room earlier, she had remembered enough about the mechanism to make some educated guesses. The tiny probe fit the input port perfectly. The port connected to the device's circuits so the lock code sequence could be changed. That required authorized passwords and commands. So did accessing the memory, but hackers managed to get around such safeguards all the time. Annie was counting on being able to get around them, too.

Using the notepad keyboard, Annie cautiously navigated through a series of access and repair programs. The lock was simple compared to most computer systems and it didn't take long to get into the lock code program. She held her breath as she keyed the lock for a data download, then exhaled as numbers began flashing on the notepad screen. It was working, but she didn't know how many numbers were in the sequence or how long it would take to get them.

The first number stabilized as Annie set the notepad down to tackle the alarm. She stuck the wire cutters in her back pocket in case she needed them in a hurry. Then she began a methodical search of the door edges with her hand.

"Got it!" Ray sat back and wiped his hand across his forehead. "The dead bolt is unlocked."

"So fast?" Annie whispered.

Ray held up a tiny, angled Allen wrench. "This was almost as good as a key."

Annie nodded, then noticed that three stationary numbers were displayed on the notepad screen. Only a few minutes had passed, and yet Ray had already beaten the deadbolt and the computer was within a few minutes of finding the lock code. The operation was moving toward success without a hitch.

Except that I can't find anything out here that connects to the alarm. Stumped, Annie dropped her chin in her hand and stared at the door.

"The numbers stopped." Ray jumped to his feet.

Annie looked down at the small screen. Six numbers glowed green in the dark, then began to flash.

"Look!" Ray pointed to the electronic lock. "Cool. It's unlocking itself. How'd you do that?"

The code numbers lit up and chimed in sequence on the lock's digital touchpad.

"I don't know," Annie said, "but I don't like it—"

The red LED went out as a green one came on.

The lock clicked.

And the alarm blared.

CHAPTER 11

Alex waited—patiently and without panicking. She was sure Annie had gotten the message and was working on a plan to rescue her. It was just a matter of time.

But the minutes had started to drag.

When I get out of this I will never complain about being bored again, Alex resolved.

Although the sound was muffled by the heavy freezer door, Alex heard the alarm.

The emergency door.

Alex listened as the seconds ticked by. The alarm on the emergency door blared every time the door was opened so no one could sneak in or out. When that happened, it kept ringing until someone turned it off. However, the alarm also rang when someone unlocked the door. The lock code triggered the alarm to test the system. Opening and closing the door during the programmed test shut it down.

The clanging stopped.

Someone had unlocked the door. But who?

Finally, Alex heard voices.

"How lucky can you get? I never expected the alarm to just shut off like that."

Ray! Yes!

"We're not out of this, yet, Ray. The police are probably on their way right now to see why it went off in the first place."

The dark freezer filled with light as the door flew open. Annie and Ray stepped into the doorway and stared at her. Both of them were wearing dark clothes and had bags hanging from their shoulders.

"Alex?" Annie took a tentative step forward and gently placed her hand on Alex's frozen body.

Yes! It's me! Alex shouted in her mind. She couldn't do anything else. Whatever happened next was up to Annie and Ray.

Ray leaned in for a closer look and waved his hand in front of her frozen face. "Yo, Alex! How'd you manage to get yourself into this mess?"

Later, Ray. It's a long story. Just get me out of here!

"She's not exactly in any condition to answer, Ray," Annie said as she set her bag down outside the freezer.

"But she can hear us, right?"

Loud and clear.

"Well, we know she saw us earlier, so she can probably hear, too. Come on. Let's get her out of this freezer."

Dropping his bag, Ray threw his arms around Alex's frozen shoulders and tilted her. "Man! She weighs a ton!"

Thanks a lot, Ray.

"She doesn't weigh any more than she did before." Annie grabbed Alex by her frozen, unformed feet and grunted. "But you're right. She is kind of heavy. Whatever you do, don't drop her! I don't know what would happen if any pieces chipped off and we lost them."

Puh-leeze, don't drop me. Alex's mind filled with an image of finally morphing back to find her nose missing. Or a finger or a foot. She shook off the grotesque pictures and stared at the floor and Ray's feet as he and Annie dragged her through the door. When they stood her back up by the pallets, she rocked slightly.

Whoa! Hey, guys!

Annie reached out to steady her, then closed the freezer door and picked up both bags. She handed one to Ray. "We can't carry her out to the car, Ray. It'll take too long."

Ray nodded and looked around. "One of those dollies should do the trick." Shouldering his bag, he ran across the room to get it.

Alex watched because she was facing in that direction. Then she heard a distant, high-pitched sound like sirens. Annie and Ray didn't seem to hear it, though. She wondered if her sense of hearing had temporarily improved. Sound had been her only source of outside input because she had been frozen in the dark.

And it sounds like the sirens are getting closer. . . .

Annie and Ray both looked up with stricken expressions.

They *were* getting closer! Alex remembered the police escort the PVCP trucks had arrived with that afternoon. She mentally yelled a warning. *The plant!*

"The plant!" Annie yelled.

"Or the cops!" Ray ducked behind a tower of stacked pallets loaded with bagged dog food.

Both.

Alex heard a truck pull up to the loading dock, groaning in low gear. A siren wailed, then whined down as a police cruiser screeched to a halt behind the truck.

Annie looked at Alex frantically. "I've got to hide! I won't be able to help you if I get caught. Understand?"

So stop talking and hide!

Mr. Lindsey burst through the double doors and headed straight for the loading dock.

Annie darted behind the empty pallets by the freezer.

Alex just sat there as the manager unlocked the large sliding door and rolled it up into the ceiling.

Lars stormed inside and stopped dead, his steely gaze fastened on Alex. His voice boomed through the storeroom as he pointed toward her.

"What is *that?*"

Alex watched a droplet of ooze form on her frozen face.

Doomed, she thought dismally.

She was already starting to melt.

CHAPTER 12

Alex shifted her attention to the horrified expression on Mr. Lindsey's face.

"I told you not to let anyone open the freezer." Lars glared at the manager.

"Nobody did!" Mr. Lindsey insisted. "That was not out here when I closed up!"

Uh-oh. If they suspect someone broke in, they'll find Annie and Ray!

Dave hopped onto the loading dock, opened the back of the refrigerated truck and disappeared inside.

The chemist shook his head in disgust. "Obviously someone in your store thought it would

be fun to see if an ice block would melt over-
night. A lot of kids work here."

"And none of them would deliberately defy
my orders or Ms. Atron's," Mr. Lindsey re-
plied hotly.

Alex really appreciated the store manager's
faith in his young employees, but she hoped Lars
wasn't convinced. If the chemist thought a kid
was to blame, Annie and Ray would be safe.

Dave rushed out of the truck with a dolly and
paused beside the chemist.

Lars looked at him and frowned. "What are
you waiting for, Dave? Get those ice blocks
loaded."

"Right." Dave ran toward the freezer.

Alex mentally flinched as the driver came to
an abrupt halt in front of her. The platform on
the bottom of the dolly just missed jamming into
her. She heard Annie inhale sharply from behind
the pallets, but Dave didn't seem to have heard.

"Not that one, Dave!" Lars began to walk
over. "Get the blocks from the freezer first while
I figure out what to do with this one."

Just leave me here, Alex thought hopefully as
the chemist paused to study her. *I'm totally use-
less to your experiment now.*

"It's all lumpy," Lars said. "Like it started to melt, then froze again."

"Maybe it did," Mr. Lindsey said. "But it didn't happen in *my* store."

Lars didn't seem to care where the ice had melted anymore. His face furrowed in thought.

The store manager squinted and looked Alex up and down. "It looks kind of like a person."

Dave glanced at her as he came out of the freezer with an ice block. "It does, doesn't it?"

Knock it off, you guys! Don't give Lars any ideas.

Alex waited, mentally crossing her fingers. Fortunately, the chemist didn't have much of an imagination and didn't see the resemblance. Unfortunately, his scientific curiosity was working at full capacity.

"Since this one is already thawing, we'll just let it keep thawing back to the plant." Lars smiled. "Might be rather interesting, actually. Can we borrow one of your dollies, Mr. Lindsey?"

"I've got two, Mr. Fredrickson. I'll give you a hand."

Cold fear gripped Alex's mind as another drop of ooze slid slowly over her face. She had frozen solid very quickly—a lot faster than ordinary water. Maybe she was defrosting faster, too!

Alex glanced at the pallets, hoping Annie was already hatching another plan. Her thoughts were rudely interrupted as Lars shoved a dolly underneath her.

Help! Alex silently cried out as the dolly tilted. She fell back against three vertical metal bars and felt herself slip toward the left side. *Don't let me fall off!*

She didn't fall. Suddenly, she was being bumped and jolted as the chemist rushed her across the storeroom, into the truck, and dumped her. Alex landed with a *thunk* that made the melted liquid sheen on her body shimmer. However, Lars had already turned his back to go get another ice block and didn't see the odd reaction.

Facing toward the open dock door, Alex was able to watch as the three men hurried to finish loading the ice blocks. A police officer stood off to the side, checking the time and looking totally bored. The last thing she saw before Dave closed the truck doors was Ray's worried face looking out from behind the dog food.

Then pitch-black darkness enveloped her again.

*   *   *

Annie didn't move while the store manager locked the loading dock doors. She waited anxiously, hoping he wouldn't decide to check the break room emergency door. He didn't. He walked quickly and directly across the room and through the swinging doors.

Annie waited another minute to make sure he was gone, then skirted the wall to reach Ray.

"We were so close!" Ray was both shaken and angry. "What are we gonna do now?"

Annie's eyes narrowed and she set her jaw. "Get out of here and go after that truck."

Moving quietly, Annie led the way into the break room and paused by the door. She pulled her keys out of her pocket and separated out the ignition key. The door was still unlocked, but the alarm would go off again as soon as it opened. If the manager was still in the store, he'd come running to check it. Once they went through the door, they had to be in the car and gone fast!

"Ready?"

Ray nodded.

They pushed through the door and ran to the end of the building with the alarm blasting in their ears. Annie stumbled to a halt and almost fell forward when Ray bumped into her. Holding up a hand, she peeked around the corner.

The manager was standing by his car. Throwing up his hands, Mr. Lindsey searched for a key as he trudged back to open the automatic doors. He wasn't in a hurry and obviously thought the alarm had been triggered by accident.

As soon as he disappeared inside, Annie and Ray ran to the car. Annie threw her bag in the back, slid inside, and had the key in the ignition in forty-five seconds flat. Both doors slammed closed simultaneously. Shoving the car into gear, Annie jammed on the gas. The car shot across the empty parking lot and squealed to a stop at the street.

"There they go!" Ray pointed toward the intersection to the right.

Siren blaring, the police car turned left when the traffic light turned green. The truck followed.

The car fishtailed slightly as Annie turned onto the empty street. She played the steering wheel and quickly straightened it out, surprising herself as well as Ray.

"Whoa, Annie!" Ray gripped the handhold as the car sped forward.

The traffic light flashed yellow.

Annie thought about barreling through it, then saw a car coming down the cross street. She slammed on the brakes as the light turned red, throwing them both forward against their seat belts.

"Take it easy, Annie. It's not like we don't know where they're going." Ray shifted in his seat but didn't let go of the handhold. "We can't rescue Alex if you have an accident and we end up in the hospital."

"Sorry, Ray, but if we don't get Alex soon, we won't get her at all."

"I don't see the problem. We've snuck into the plant a dozen times before. We'll just wait and take her out of the freezer after everyone leaves."

"Lars isn't putting her in the freezer." Ray, Annie realized, hadn't been close enough to hear the conversation in the storeroom. "She's already starting to thaw and I think she's thawing at an accelerated rate."

The light changed and Annie turned left. The truck was still visible several blocks ahead. Driving as fast as she dared to keep up, Annie told Ray her theory concerning the chemist's *real* reason for freezing sunflowers. It was only the first step toward freezing people.

"By my calculations, Alex will be turning into slush in an hour—give or take a few minutes. It'll take at least that long to get all the ice blocks inside. Lars is bound to notice something odd and he'll be too intrigued to leave. He'll wait and watch—"

"—until Alex materializes." Ray turned slowly to stare at Annie. "Alive and well after being frozen."

"So our best chance is to snatch her from the truck *before* they take her into the plant."

Nodding, Ray looked out the windshield. "The truck's turning again."

"So's that light." Muttering in frustration, Annie stopped the car and drummed her fingers on the steering wheel. Waiting was hard with adrenaline coursing through her veins and her frozen sister trapped in a truck.

When the light changed, Annie pushed the speed limit to get to the next corner. The light turned yellow as she reached the intersection. No other cars were in sight. She turned and accelerated up a rise. When the car reached the top, Annie and Ray both gasped.

A convoy of four identical refrigerated trucks

and police cars sped toward the plant on the road ahead.

"Which one is she in? They all look the same!"

"I don't know, Ray." Annie drove on, lost in grim, silent thought for a minute before she had an idea. "Dave! We just have to find the truck Dave's driving."

"That shouldn't be too hard," Ray said. "But we've got to catch them first."

Annie pulled up behind the last truck in line as the convoy began turning onto the plant grounds. However, there was extra security at the shipping-and-receiving gate checking employee IDs. Annie didn't have a legitimate reason to be there. In fact, she didn't want anyone to know she had entered the plant. Driving on up the road, she turned around and went back to the visitors parking lot in front of the administration building.

Annie used her father's ID code to enter the main complex through a side entrance. She did not want her own ID code on record. If something went wrong getting Alex out, the access records could be checked to see which employees had come in. Her father had been called back to work. He was supposed to be there.

Moving through the complex on foot without being seen took longer than Annie had figured, too. By the time they reached the parking area by the research and development labs, the trucks were already backed up to unload.

And the drivers were no longer in their cabs. They were already rushing into the building with ice blocks.

Annie and Ray hid behind some thick bushes next to the building and watched.

"There's Dave," Ray hissed. The driver dashed into the second truck from the end closest to them. "Okay. Now we know which truck, but we'll never get her out without those guys seeing us."

Ray was right, Annie realized with a sinking heart, but it wasn't a problem anymore.

Dave raced out of the truck with Alex on his dolly.

They were too late.

CHAPTER 13

Alex was *really* getting tired of being treated like a block of ice. The ride in the truck had been rough. Every time Dave turned a corner, she had been sure she was going to topple over and smash. Then she would have had a lot more than a missing nose to worry about!

Dave had not been exactly gentle when he scooped her onto the dolly, either. And now, as though her dignity hadn't suffered enough, he was racing another driver down the corridor— and losing!

At least the floors in here are smooth, Alex thought as she sped by empty offices, storerooms, and labs. But her troubles were far from over.

Alex fought back a rush of anxiety as Dave slowed before crashing into a large door that connected the labs to the administration building. She glanced through the open door on her right. The walls were lined with shelves and cabinets. A supply room.

Dave turned left, following the other driver into a lab full of stainless steel counters, cabinets, and equipment.

"Here's the lumpy one you wanted, Mr. Fredrickson."

Standing by a freezer across the room, the chemist waved his clipboard at the corner by the door. "Just put it there for now."

Dave pushed Alex into the corner and slid her off the dolly—facing a cabinet attached to the wall.

Alex stared at her reflection in the glass door and indulged in feeling sorry for herself for one minute. She *was* lumpy, but she wouldn't be for long. Another small glob of defrosted ooze slid over her frozen face. The thawing had slowed down while she was in the refrigerated truck, but it was speeding up again. And now that she was inside Lars's lab, Annie's chances of getting her out before she melted completely were almost zero.

Minute's up, Alex. Do something!

Alex stared at the glass cabinet door. It was the only thing she could do. However, the far wall behind her was also reflected in the shining surface. She watched Lars inspect an ice block. He made a notation on his clipboard as the driver pushed it into the freezer.

Then her father walked into view carrying a computer printout.

"I've finished logging in these specimens."

"Excellent. Here's another batch." Lars pulled the top sheet off the clipboard and handed it to Mr. Mack. "And check that one in the corner for a number."

A wave of affection swept through Alex as her dad walked over and began scanning her slick surface. *Hi, Dad.*

Mr. Mack straightened up. "I can't find the number, Lars. I think it melted off."

"No matter. We'll identify it by the process of elimination when all the blocks are logged in."

Mr. Mack hurried out the door and Lars turned back to his clipboard.

Alex watched the glass in fascinated surprise. A thin *sheet* of melted ooze rippled down her entire body and pooled around her formless feet. She was melting faster and faster. It wouldn't be long before she was slush and then a puddle. Alex didn't know if she'd have a full five minutes to stay morphed or if she'd materialize immediately. Either way, the risk of Lars seeing the change was too great to take.

I have to get out of here!

And she moved.

Alex's brain stalled for a startled moment.

Did I move or was it my imagination? Concentrating on the liquid ooze gathered around her feet, Alex tried to move again. She slid an inch to her right. She had moved! The melted ooze supporting her frozen bulk was acting like a roller. She couldn't move too far too fast, but zipping across the floor wasn't a good idea, anyway. Not with Lars in the room.

Still, the chemist wasn't paying close attention to her. Maybe she could inch her way to the door. It was only a few feet away. Then she could scoot across the hall and hide in the supply room. However, once she moved away from the cabinet, she wouldn't be able to see behind her in the glass anymore.

About face!

Inch by inch, Alex slowly turned herself around. The maneuver took several minutes because she had to stop each time the drivers rushed in and out the door. Finally, she was facing the interior of the lab. She waited a moment, then sluggishly moved a few more inches.

Lars looked up suddenly and scowled.

Alex paused, tense and nervous as his gaze swept the room. Shaking his head, the chemist looked back at his clipboard.

Another sheet of liquid flowed down her body toward the floor. Then the lower part of her collapsed slightly.

Huh? Puzzled, Alex cautiously slid another few inches toward the door. Dave entered and stopped at the same instant she did. He scratched his head and continued on to the freezer. Then Alex felt herself *sink* to the left.

What's happening now? Suddenly, Alex realized that her insides were thawing, too! Just not as quickly as her outside. Her interior was colder than her surface because it wasn't directly exposed to the warm environment. As she turned to icy slush, her lower parts couldn't support her frozen weight. She was shrinking!

Lars and Dave had their backs turned toward her. Aware that every second counted now, Alex crawled another foot toward the door. Then another and another. Just one more foot and she'd be out—

Dave wheeled his dolly around and headed back to the door.

"And don't dawdle. This will be the last one." Lars glared after Dave, then walked into the freezer.

Alex felt her defrosting self tremble. Dave was sure to notice that she wasn't in the same spot she had been a moment ago. She *crunched* as her weight settled again.

Dave did a double take as he drew closer. He hesitated, glanced back at the freezer, shrugged, then kept going through the door.

Thank you, Dave! Apparently, the driver just wanted to finish his job and go home without upsetting the chemist again.

Cruunnch!

I'm out of here! Alex couldn't afford to wait now. Lars's attention wouldn't be totally focused on the other ice blocks after Dave delivered the last one. And the chemist wouldn't ignore the incredible, shrinking ice block in the corner.

Desperately hoping that Lars would stay in the freezer another minute, Alex zipped the last twelve inches to the door. The more she melted, the faster she was able to slide. She hesitated just long enough to check the hall. Dave disappeared around the corner at the far end. She heard the muted sound of engines starting as the other drivers prepared to leave. Safety was just across the hall.

Alex zoomed out the door.

The heavy door into the administration building flew open and Annie jumped out in front of her.

Alex put on the brakes, but couldn't stop. Annie reached out with her hands, turned her and shoved her through the door that Ray was holding open. Propelled by the extra momentum of Annie's push, Alex slid down the corridor out of control. Annie and Ray raced after her.

"Hey!" Lars's voice echoed through the heavy door as it swung closed. "Where's my melted ice block?"

"Maybe it melted—" Dave's voice was cut off as the door clunked shut.

"Which way?" Ray asked as he and Annie chased Alex toward intersecting hallways.

I don't know about you, but I'm going straight ahead! Alex couldn't get traction on the hard polished floors. She thought it might be because the liquid ooze she rolled on was still colder than normal. Or maybe because she had no control over her bulk that was still half-frozen—which was most of her.

"Left!" Annie hissed loudly.

Ray caught up to Alex just before she entered the junction of corridors. Placing his hands on her mushy head, he steered her in a wide curve and sent her careening down the hall to the left. Annie skidded around the corner and quickly closed the distance between them.

"It's not in the supply room!" Dave hollered.

"This way, Dave!" Lars's voice bellowed down the hall they had just left. "Someone stole that ice block and I'm gonna find out who!"

"Why would anyone want it?" Dave asked.

"To ruin my project! No one's left in the building except those guys who think they're my scientific equals!"

He's right about that, Alex thought as she slid down the long corridor between Annie and Ray.

The offices were all closed and the hallway was deserted—

Except for Dad and his coworkers!

Several yards ahead, Alex saw part of someone's back sticking out of an office doorway. Ray and Annie both gasped softly. *With good reason,* Alex thought. If they went back, they would run right into Lars and Dave. If they went forward, the man in the door would spot them. He could probably already hear them running. Her father's office was just ahead—but he was in it!

The man in the doorway spoke up. "You two go on home."

Dad? Above her, Alex saw Annie and Ray exchange glances. She had shrunk to about half-size now and her slushy body made a slurping sound as she moved. But her morphed vision was almost back to normal.

"I'll finish this up," Mr. Mack said. "There's no reason for everyone to stay past midnight."

"Thanks, George!" Two men inside the office said.

Working in perfect unison, Annie and Ray instantly steered Alex to the left and into her father's office.

And just in the nick of time. Alex could distinctly

hear her father's heels clicking on the floor as he walked back down the hall. Lars and Dave were running from the opposite direction.

Ray jumped to the closet and opened the door. He rushed inside behind Alex and Annie and eased the door closed just before Mr. Mack walked into the office.

At least, I'm not in this alone anymore, Alex thought as she huddled in the dark with Annie and Ray. They had taken some very dangerous chances trying to rescue her. There was no way she could adequately express how much she appreciated their efforts, but she couldn't wait until she had her voice back so she could try.

For the moment, Alex was satisfied knowing they were all safe. Now they just had to wait until she was completely thawed so she could materialize. Then, after her father was gone, they could all just walk out and go home.

"I'd like a word with you, George."

Alex *felt* Annie and Ray tense as Lars stomped into the office.

"I'm almost done with these entries," Mr. Mack said. "Is that the last tally sheet?"

"Yes, but that's not why I'm here," the chemist

said bluntly. "One of the ice blocks is missing and you were the last person to touch it. So you won't mind if I have a look in your closet, will you, George?"

"Why, no . . . but it's not there."

Oh, yes it is!

CHAPTER 14

"Ummphhh." Alex grunted as Ray leaned over her and clutched the doorknob. Annie flinched.

Fine time to find my voice! Alex struggled to stay calm. In about two seconds, Lars was going to open the closet door and make the scientific discovery of a lifetime. *And the rest of* my *lifetime will be totally destroyed.*

Ray braced himself, but Alex realized his plan wouldn't work. He wasn't strong enough to keep the door from moving when the chemist tried to pull it open. The door would give a little, then snap back—a dead giveaway that someone was inside trying to hold it closed.

"Could I have that list, please?" Mr. Mack asked.

Alex heard paper rustle, then footsteps.

Act now or forfeit!

Crunching and slurping, Alex forced some of her slushy self under the door to wedge it tightly closed. She hoped Lars hadn't heard her and that none of her semimelted ooze was sticking out on the other side.

Her father's computer keyboard clicked in the background as he continued making his data entries.

Ray tightened his grip on the doorknob as it started to turn and held it firmly.

The chemist yanked on the knob, but the door didn't budge.

"Is this locked?" Lars asked.

"No," Mr. Mack said shortly. "Here's the key."

The keys jingled as they were tossed and caught. The lock rattled as the chemist inserted a key and turned it. But the door didn't move when he tried to open it again.

"It must be stuck," Lars muttered.

"I could get a crowbar," Dave offered.

"That won't be necessary." Mr. Mack's voice was firm. "All the ice blocks are accounted for."

"What?" The chemist sounded surprised.

"I've entered all the numbers you gave us and I just ran a cross-check. None of the numbers are missing. So none of your ice blocks are missing, either." Mr. Mack's voice was infused with a touch of triumph. "That melted block didn't have a number, remember?"

Way to go, Dad! Alex flushed with pride for her brilliant father.

Lars coughed. "Are you saying that I've been worrying about a block of ordinary *grocery store* ice?"

"No, Lars," Mr. Mack said calmly. "*I* wouldn't say that."

But it's true and you know it, Lars. Although, I'm not exactly ordinary *ice.* Alex had to hold back a giggle.

Lars sighed. "But where did that ice go?"

"It probably melted, like I said," Dave suggested.

"Excuse me, gentlemen," Mr. Mack said. "I'm going home."

"But there wasn't any water on the floor," Lars muttered as he walked out.

"Well, one thing's for sure. It didn't get up and walk away by itself. . . ." Dave's voice faded as he followed the scientists out of the office.

Annie listened at the door, then finally motioned Ray to open it. "Let's get moving."

"Ah'm sstilll frooo-zenn." Alex started at the deep, drawn-out sound of her half-frozen morphed voice. She sounded like one of her father's old forty-five-rpm records played at slow speed under water.

Annie and Ray stared at her and Alex could tell they were trying not to laugh.

"We've got to go now, guys," Annie said. "I don't want to explain to Dad where I've been with the car so late. If we hurry, we can get home first."

"No problem the way you're driving lately, Annie." Ray looked at Alex. "Besides, I really don't want to hang around here."

Alex didn't, either.

Moving faster now that she was a pile of slush, Alex didn't have any trouble keeping up with Annie and Ray as they raced out of the building and across the deserted parking lot. They had a tense moment when Mr. Mack, who was leaving from the employee parking lot, drove by right before they pulled onto the street. However, he was so intent on getting home, his gaze was riveted on the road.

Annie took a shortcut through a residential section. Although she didn't break any traffic laws, she didn't waste any time, either. Alex sloshed back and forth in the backseat whenever they turned a corner because she couldn't strap in, but her form held together.

Annie pulled into the driveway just as another car turned onto their street a block away. There was a light on in the living room, but the upstairs windows were dark.

"Mission accomplished!" Ray said as he jumped out of the car and opened the back door for Alex.

Alex plopped onto the pavement and desperately tried to materialize. She couldn't. There were still ice crystals in her system.

"This isn't over, yet." Annie tossed Ray his bag and shouldered her own. "Through the garage. Hurry."

Alex and Ray didn't need any urging. They reached the side door in seconds, then both shifted impatiently as Annie put the key in the lock.

Mr. Mack's car turned into the drive.

Annie opened the door and flipped the light switch on. Nobody argued when she started giving orders. They didn't have time.

"Ray! Go turn on the TV."

Ray bolted through the kitchen door for the living room.

"You better stay here, Alex." Annie shoved her bag under the train table. "Just until you materialize. Dad'll probably go right to bed, anyway. It's almost one."

"O-kay," Alex gurgled.

As Annie started to open the door into the kitchen, Mr. Mack walked into the garage through the side door.

Sshhh-loop! Alex slithered under the train table with the speed of a stretched elastic band being released.

"Dad!" Annie paled.

"Hi, Annie." Mr. Mack dropped a bag of car litter in a trash can, then walked to the door. "You're working late tonight, too, huh?"

"Uh—yeah. Kinda."

Uh-oh. Alex felt a warm, tingling sensation begin to course through her. She was going to materialize any second.

Annie opened the kitchen door.

"Are you hungry?" Mr. Mack paused in the doorway.

"Starved! Hey, Mr. Mack!" Ray grabbed a bag of chips off the counter and dashed back to the living room.

"What's Ray doing here at this hour?"

"Watching movies—with Alex," Annie said. "It's Friday night."

"Oh, right." Mr. Mack stepped into the kitchen.

Annie followed him and closed the door.

Now!

A rush of warm tingles and one hot flash later, Alex crawled out from under the table with the cake box under her arm. It looked a little squashed. She peeked under the lid, rolled her eyes, and tucked the lid flap back in.

Feeling stiff, Alex stood up and went to the door. She cracked it cautiously, but no one was in the kitchen. Zapping the garage light off, she darted inside to stash the cake. Her father came back in just as she closed the freezer door.

Mr. Mack stopped in surprise. "Where'd you come from?"

"Oh, I just pop up in the strangest places."

"What's strange about the kitchen?" Wearing a long robe, Mrs. Mack paused in the doorway and kissed Mr. Mack on the cheek. Then she stretched and yawned. "You must be exhausted, George."

"Actually, I'm hungry."

"After that huge dinner you ate?" Mrs. Mack asked.

"That was hours ago."

Alex moved out of the way as Mr. Mack started for the refrigerator.

Mrs. Mack stopped him and ushered him to the table. "Have I got a surprise for you!"

"What?" Mr. Mack's eyes sparkled with anticipation.

"A french vanilla ice cream chocolate cake!"

"Cake?" Annie gasped from the doorway.

"I'm ready." Standing behind Annie, Ray grinned. The grin faded as he glanced at Alex. "I think."

"It's in the freezer." Alex smiled and winked at Annie. "I said I'd bring it home and I did. Safe and—frozen."

"You are a truly amazing person, Alex Mack." Annie nodded, then motioned for Alex to follow her into the living room. The two sisters hugged, then Annie plopped down on the sofa.

"How did you manage to get frozen, Alex?"

Shaking her head, Alex sat beside Annie on the couch. "I had to morph to get the cake and it took longer than I expected. I didn't do it on purpose."

"I didn't think so, but this accidental freezing experiment of yours might have side effects. I want to know every single detail you can remember—no matter how trivial it seems."

"I knew you were going to ask me that, but"— Alex yawned—"not tonight. After what I went through to bring that cake home, I'm going to have a piece. Then I'm going to bed. I have to work tomorrow."

"But you've got to tell me now—while it's all still fresh in your mind. You might forget something important."

Alex smiled. "Believe me, Annie. I won't forget."

Not in a million years.

About the Author

Diana G. Gallagher lives in Kansas with her husband Marty Burke, two dogs, three cats, and a cranky parrot. When she's not writing, she likes to read and take long walks with the dogs.

A Hugo Award–winning illustrator, she is best known for her series *Woof: The House Dragon.* Her songs about humanity's future are sung throughout the world and have been recorded in cassette form: "Cosmic Concepts More Complete," "Star*Song," and "Fire Dream." Diana and Marty, an Irish folksinger, perform traditional and original music at science-fiction conventions.

Her first adult novel, *The Alien Dark,* appeared in 1990. She is also the author of a *Star Trek: Deep Space Nine*® novel for young readers, *Arcade,* and several other books in *The Secret World of Alex Mack* series, all available from Minstrel Books.

She is currently working on another *Star Trek* novel and *Alex Mack* story.